Please return on or before the latest date above.
You can renew online at *www.kent.gov.uk/libs*
or by telephone 08458 247 200

HARPER, FIONA
SWEPT OFF HER
STILETTOS

AF/LP
01/12

C155313509

CUSTOMER SERVICE EXCELLENCE

Libraries & Archives

00884\DTP\RN\07.07   LIB 7

SWEPT OFF
HER STILETTOS

SWEPT OFF HER STILETTOS

BY

FIONA HARPER

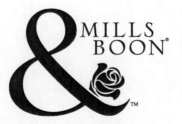

First published in Great Britain 2011
by Mills & Boon, an imprint of Harlequin (UK) Limited.
Large Print edition 2011
Harlequin (UK) Limited, Eton House,
18-24 Paradise Road, Richmond, Surrey TW9 1SR

© Fiona Harper 2011

ISBN: 978 0 263 22254 8

Harlequin (UK) policy is to use papers that are natural,
renewable and recyclable products and made from
wood grown in sustainable forests. The logging and
manufacturing process conform to the legal environmental
regulations of the country of origin.

Printed and bound in Great Britain
by CPI Antony Rowe, Chippenham, Wiltshire

For Gillian Constance Johnson
(1941–2010),
a cool chick and a loving mum.

CHAPTER ONE

The Girl Can't Help It...

Coreen's Confessions
No.1—In my opinion, a pinkie finger isn't properly dressed unless it's got a man comfortably wrapped around it—and I always make sure I'm impeccably dressed.

I GLARED at the man who'd rushed through the coffee shop door. Not only had he almost spilled my caramel mochaccino down my best polka-dot dress as he'd barged past, but he hadn't even bothered to hold the door open for me.

Not that I was about to admit I was losing my mojo. He probably just hadn't seen me in his rush to escape from the unseasonable weather.

Left with no alternative, I balanced the two steaming paper cups of coffee I was holding and tried to open the door with my elbow. No good.

There was only one thing for it. I sighed, turned one-eighty degrees, and shoved it open with my rear end.

I glanced upwards as I stepped outside onto Greenwich High Street. The sky wasn't just promising rain but threatening with menaces. What should have been a balmy summer evening was as heavy and gloomy as a December afternoon. Thankfully, I only had a two-minute walk ahead of me, and would be safe and dry inside before the heavens opened.

Rude Man had something else to answer for too. No one would be standing with his hand on the open door, transfixed, as a steady stream of customers flowed past him. No one would be admiring my rear view as I walked away, my head high and my hips swaying like Marilyn's in *Some Like It Hot*. I'd watched that movie at least fifty times before I'd got the walk down pat, and the least I deserved was a little appreciation for my efforts.

I squared my shoulders and lifted my chin. Well, I was going to make the journey back to the shop count—rude man or no rude man. There was plenty of traffic passing by to serve as an audience. I placed one red patent stiletto in front of the other and began to walk.

I nipped round the corner into Church Street and then across the busy junction into Nelson Street. However, not even the sight its neat row of cream Georgian buildings lifted my mood this evening. Normally when I passed each shop or boutique I'd smile and wave at the owner as I counted down the door numbers with growing excitement.

On the corner was the all-organic coffee shop—closed now, but mid-morning packed with Yummy Mummies who cluttered the floor space with their high-tech pushchairs and the air with discussions on the merits of the local private nurseries. Next was the second-hand bookshop that did a roaring trade in textbooks for the students at the nearby university campus. After that was Susie's—a bakery that specialised entirely in cupcakes. The window was full of frosted and glittering towers of different flavoured cakes, delicious-looking enough to cause even the most dedicated dieter to stop and lick her lips. Then there was a Thai restaurant, a newsagent's, and a shop called Petal that sold just about anything as long as it was pink.

Finally, next door to that, two doors down from the end of the eclectic row, was my shop—Coreen's Closet—a vintage clothing emporium to rival the best in London.

I was in an even worse mood by the time I pushed the shop door open and flipped the sign to 'Closed'.

Not a single honk or whistle as I'd made my journey! Another first. I didn't want to give my recent doubts credit, but this didn't bode well.

'What's got you in a snit?' Alice said as I plonked her decaff latte on the counter. My business partner was one of those ethereal-looking types—flame-red hair, pale skin, willowy figure. Well, not so willowy at present. She was seven months pregnant, and being such a slip of a thing there was only one way that baby bump could go—outwards. She looked as if, python-like, she'd swallowed my classic VW Beetle for breakfast.

I prised the plastic lid off my mochaccino and blew on it. 'There's something wrong with the male population of London today.'

Alice chuckled. She knew me too well.

Despite my best attempts to pout, the corner of my mouth curled up. I took a sip of my coffee, then smiled back at her. She was leaning on the counter for support, circling her swollen ankles.

'Crikey, Alice! You look dead on your feet.'

She gave me a hooded look. 'Gee, thanks.'

I put my cup on the counter and trotted off into the back room. When I returned I presented Alice with her umbrella and handbag. 'You need to get home. Call Cameron. I can manage the stock-take on my own.'

She started to protest, but I wouldn't allow it. I fished her mobile out of her bag, pressed the button for her husband's speed-dial and then handed her the phone when I heard it ringing at the other end. Within fifteen minutes her adorably protective husband had picked her up and taken her home to run her a bath, fuss over her, and generally indulge her every hormone-induced whim.

That's what men are for, really, aren't they?

Oh, I didn't mean hormones and morning sickness! I'm not ready for that yet. Not by a long shot. The whim-catering bit? *That* I'm all for.

Once the door was locked behind Alice, I marched into the office at the back, grabbed my purple glittery clipboard and set to work. It wasn't usually a chore. I loved my little treasure trove of vintage clothes and accessories. Some days I thought it was a tragedy to unlock the shop door and let other people leave with the fabulousness that I amass in my limited square footage. But a girl's gotta keep herself in lipstick and stockings somehow.

I worked my way through the clothing racks as the weather-induced twilight deepened outside. Every now and then a group of students trailed past the shop window, off into the town centre in search of cheap food and even cheaper beer, but other than that the street was deserted. The fashionable bistros and wine bars would start to hum in an hour or so, but until then there was no one walking by to marvel at how the beaded handbags and evening gowns in my window display gathered the light from the rear of the shop and threw it back into the street in multi-coloured droplets.

I sat down on the varnished floorboards between the heaving clothing rails, the skirt of my red-and-white polka-dot dress spreading around me in a perfect circle, and pushed away a stray dark hair that had worked its way out of my neat quiff. Shoes were next, and I started checking the pairs on a low rack off my list.

I grabbed a pair of silver platform boots and checked the size and condition. I might have been tempted to adopt them, but although I do dress that way for fun sometimes, really I'm a Fifties girl at heart.

By today's size-zero culture my figure's considered too full...too lacking in visibly defined muscle...too pale with not even a hint of spray-on tan. My curves belong to another time—a time when red-lipped sirens winked saucily from the side of aeroplanes, when the perfect shape for a woman was considered to be an hourglass, not an *emery board*, for goodness' sake.

Unwisely, I'd tucked one leg underneath myself, and it didn't take long before it went to sleep. I unhooked it and shook it around. In the quiet shop my net petticoat rustled, drowning out the sound of the rain that had just begun peppering the large plate-glass window.

I put the boots back on the rack, leaving the

sparkly purple clipboard and pen on the floor beside me untouched, and picked up a darling evening shoe with a starched bow on the toe. For some reason I just stared at it. Not that it wasn't stare-worthy, but I was staring without really seeing. And then I realised I hadn't ticked the silver boots off my list, so I dropped the shoe into my lap and picked up my pen.

I sighed. I wasn't getting the usual joy this evening from the velvet and satin, from the whisper-soft silk lingerie. What was wrong with me? I'd achieved everything I'd worked for in the last few years. No more standing around draughty market stalls, stamping my feet and cursing the English weather. Coreen's Closet was bricks and mortar now and, thanks to a rather successful joint venture with Alice's husband, we were the happening new vintage shop in south London.

As well as the faithful customers who'd followed me from the market stall, I'd managed to attract some of the hot young socialites who thought vintage was cooler than cool, and who'd pay vast amounts for anything by a classic designer. I'd got the best of both worlds, really. Everything I'd planned and scrimped and saved for.

So why wasn't I lindy-hopping round my clothes racks, whooping as I went, instead of sitting on the floor counting the same pair of boots over and over again?

Maybe it was because I usually did this job with Alice. It was kind of quiet in here without her. I missed the gossip and the shared thrill of finding some fabulous skirt or blouse we'd forgotten about, squished amongst the other clothes. But Alice's absence tonight was just a symptom of another disturbing change in my life.

I once used to be the centre of a large gang of single gals, all footloose and fancy-free, but I was the odd one out now. They were all paired up, more interested in painting nurseries than painting the town red. It could make a girl feel, well...lonely. Left behind. And that was a state I was definitely not comfortable with. I'd seen what Left Behind did to a person.

I wasn't jealous, though. Really I wasn't.

I tested myself. I imagined owning a little red-brick house and coming home to the same face every evening, cooking the dinner, paying the bills... No. It didn't appeal. It was too staid. Too ordinary. People stagnated like that, and there was only one of two ways it could end: either they both numbed themselves to the dreariness and put up with each other, or one morning one of them woke up to discover the other side of the bed permanently empty, a note of dubious apology on the mantel, and a piece of themselves missing, accidentally packed in haste by the departed one, along with the wrong toothbrush and a stray sock.

So, no. I wasn't jealous. Not in the slightest.

That sounded really snobby, didn't it? As if I was belittling what my friends had found. But it wasn't like that. I just wanted…

I didn't really know what I wanted. I couldn't identify what the nagging little ache inside me was, but every time it made itself known it reminded me of going into my favourite coffee shop, ravenous and ready to devour something sweet, only to look in the display case stuffed full of pastries and cakes and realise that nothing would hit the spot. It was all very unsettling.

I looked down at my chest, impressively showcased in the sweetheart neckline of my dress. My curves had arrived early in my life, and it hadn't taken long to cotton on to the fact that men were simple creatures: easily brought to a drooling standstill with the right kind of encouragement. An ample chest and a well-timed pout can get a girl just about anything she wants.

However, I was starting to think I was losing my touch, and the events of this evening had only served to deepen my fears on that front. Because the truth was…there was one man who seemed to be immune to me, even though I'd given him every bit of my best *encouragement*.

I sighed and stared at the silver boots. The box beside their description on my list remained empty. Tickless.

The stupid stray bit of hair was back again, tickling my cheek and generally mocking me. I shook it out of the way and somehow that small gesture brought me back to reality.

I was being daft. There was nothing wrong with me. Just this morning a man walking behind me had spilled hot coffee over himself as I'd bent down to open the shutter over the front door. That didn't sound like I was losing my mojo, now, did it?

I grabbed my clipboard, marked the boots off my list and added a little comment about the heel height, and then I got that pesky hair and shoved it under one of my hairgrips, pinning it away and out of sight with the rest of my maudlin thoughts.

I was halfway through my inventory of hats and hair accessories when a tapping on the window magnified, becoming more insistent. At first I hardly registered it, thinking somewhere in the back of my head that it was just the rain, but eventually I realised that even London rain couldn't be *that* persistent.

I ignored it anyway. Honestly! It was after seven. The 'Closed' sign on the door wasn't just a hint, you know. But, knowing our internet, everything-at-a-click generation, even that wouldn't be enough for some would-be customers.

I stood up, brushed my skirt down and prepared myself to make *Clear off!* and *I have a life too!* hand gestures. While I understood the obsessive nature of some of my customers—and, to be honest, I shared it a little—not having exactly the right pair of loafers for their Swing Dance class that evening could hardly be considered a 999 emergency.

I minimised my wiggle as I walked to the shop

door, hands on hips. This was one time when *encouragement* would only make things worse.

Over the top of the large 'Closed' sign I could see a pair of eyes and a scruffy brown haircut, but it was hard to make out who it was, because he was shielding his eyes with his hand in an attempt to see further into the shop. Great. One of my love-lorn swains—as my friend Jennie calls them—might just have gone all stalkerish on me again.

But then he spotted me walking towards him and pulled his hand away from his eyes and stepped back. Even in the gloom of the false twilight I could make out his broad smile. I could even see the dimples half-hidden by his light stubble.

'Adam!' I yelled, and rushed to unbolt the door.

And Adam it was, standing there in the rain with his eyes aglow and a bulging white carrier bag hanging off one of his outstretched arms.

'What are you doing here?' I said as I flung myself at him and dragged him inside. 'I thought you were in the depths of the jungle somewhere!'

'I was,' he said, disentangling himself from me,

all the while guarding the plain white carrier bag carefully. 'But now I'm back.'

The smile grew in devilish wattage, reaching its peak in his deep brown eyes. This was the smile that had half my single girlfriends begging me to set them up with him. The other half just fanned themselves down and muttered things like 'molten chocolate' and 'come to Mama' under their breaths.

Of course I never did get around to setting any of my friends up with Adam. Not that I'm not a good friend, but the situation had the potential to become far too complicated. More than one girl had accused me of being a tad territorial when it came to Adam, but really it was nothing more than good old-fashioned self-preservation—really it was.

I led Adam through to the small back office of Coreen's Closet. Now he was inside, delicious wafts of warm spice accompanied him.

'You've brought Chinese food!'

He nodded, and dumped the bag in the middle of the desk. 'I phoned Alice when I couldn't reach you at home and she told me you were here, stock-taking. I thought you'd probably be famished by now.'

Adam Conrad is one of my favourite people in the whole world. And not just because he has some weird kind of built-in radar which means he turns up with takeaway at the moment I need it the most. Even weirder—it's always the *right* kind of takeaway too. He never brings Indian when I'm in the mood for a pizza, or kebabs when I'm craving Thai. I wonder how he does it? It's a gift. Truly it is.

Adam's eyes widened as I pulled a garish pink wicker basket down from a shelf.

'Excess stock from the shop next door,' I explained as I undid the leather buckles and opened the lid to reveal a perfectly pink picnic set. 'Daisies or roses?' I said, indicating the patterned plates. Adam wrinkled his nose. The smile hadn't completely left his face ever since he'd spotted me marching towards him through the shop door, but now it creased into a grimace before popping back into place. Sometimes I swear his face must be made of elastic. It isn't natural to smile that much.

'Can't I just eat out of the carton?' he asked hopefully.

I shook my head, and he flopped down on the ancient chintz sofa on the other side of our staff-room-slash-office. He held a hand over his eyes in mock despair. 'You choose. Whichever one you think will dilute my pure masculine appeal the least.'

I snorted. 'I'm giving you daisies,' I said, with a wicked glint in my eye.

He just raised his eyebrows a little and smiled even harder. That's the thing with Adam—he's impossible to annoy. No matter how OTT I get, he's always his same laid-back, unruffled self. I used to find it annoying that I couldn't light his fuse—and, believe me, I spent a few years trying very hard to do just that—but nowadays I'm just grateful for his happy-go-lucky nature. I suppose I'm what some people would call 'high-maintenance', and in my quieter moments I know that a friend who'll put up with me twenty-four-seven is a gift from on high.

We dished out copious amounts of food with pink spoons and started to eat it with pink forks, filling each other in on news of the last month or two. We didn't usually have such a long gap between seeing each other, but he'd been away on business. More like a boys' adventure holiday paid for on the company credit card, I thought. I mean, who can claim climbing up trees and messing about with bits of rope and wood a legitimate business expense? Adam does it. And he even fills in his tax form with a straight face.

'Are you all right?'

I looked up. My fork was lying on my plate, a king prawn still speared on it. I didn't remember putting it down. 'I'm fine.'

Adam frowned slightly. 'It's just…you've been unusually quiet. For you. I've been managing to speak in whole sentences without being interrupted. It's very unnerving. And you keep sighing.'

'Do I?' Even to my own ears my voice sounded far-off and a little dazed. I decided to deflect him a little. I wasn't ready to talk with Adam about what was bugging me.

'Nan said something to me the other day…' I picked up my pink fork and doused the prawn on the end in sauce. 'She told me she thought my biological clock was ticking.'

Adam reacted just as I'd hoped he would. He erupted into fits of laughter.

I crossed my arms. 'Well, it's nonsense,' I said, feigning irritation quite passably and hoping Adam would take my rather distracting bait. 'Even if I *had* a clock—which I very much doubt—I can't hear it, and surely I'm the one who counts in this scenario?'

Adam grabbed the paper bag of sweet-and-sour pork balls off the desk and delved inside. 'That'll be the ear muffs,' he muttered, without looking up. I think he was counting the pork balls to see how many he could filch without me noticing.

I frowned and scanned the office. What on earth was he talking about? I should have been grateful, I supposed. At least it had got him off the subject of my sudden attack of glumness.

And then I spotted some—in a torn cardboard box under the desk, which was full of winter stock I hadn't cleared away properly yet. I reached forward and hooked them with my finger.

'What? *These* ear muffs?' I asked, holding a fetching baby-blue pair aloft.

Adam looked up, his mouth halfway round a crisp golden ball of batter. He bit into it and chewed slowly, not in the least perturbed by the hurry-up-and-spit-it-out vibes I was sending him. He licked his lips. 'Not exactly,' he said, keeping eye contact with me, but dipping his hand into the paper bag again. 'I was talking more about your metaphorical ear muffs—the ones you wear to stop you hearing anything you don't want to.'

My fingers tightened around the plastic band joining the two balls of fur together.

Adam just gave me a lazy smile. 'I believe there's a matching pair of polka-dotted blinkers too. Silk-lined, of course…'

He had to break off to duck out of the way of a flying pair of ear muffs. I quickly leaned forward and swiped a pork ball out of the bag with my free hand before he could stop me.

After a few seconds he narrowed his eyes. I thought he was reacting to my food-stealing counter-attack, but it turned out it was much worse.

'Just because you can't hear it, it doesn't mean the clock isn't there…that it isn't ticking…' he said.

I'd talked myself into a corner, hadn't I? Time to end this stupid discussion once and for all.

'Nan was wrong. My biological clock is *not* ticking,' I said emphatically.

'So you say…' Adam just smiled serenely at me, and then picked up the ear muffs, which had landed just beside the sofa, and jammed them on his head.

I tried to tell him just how wrong he was about this, about all the reasons why I was still the same never-be-boxed-in, never-get-boring-and-predictable Coreen he'd always known, but he just kept nodding and smiling and mouthing, 'I can't hear you!' while pointing to the ear muffs. I was sorely tempted to rip them off his head and ram them down his throat, but there's no excuse for ruining perfectly good stock, so I nicked his chow mein instead. That'd teach him.

Eventually he pulled the ear muffs off his head and threw them back to me. The impish grin flattened out slightly. 'Nah. I'm not buying it,' he said. 'Something's up with you, and it's got nothing to do with ticking clocks.'

I kept my focus on my plate and said nothing.

There was a deceptive carelessness in Adams's voice when he tried again. 'If it was anyone else I'd think it was man trouble. But I have it on good authority that there are men all over London who love nothing better than to follow you 'round like adoring puppies and scramble over each other to do your bidding every time you snap your fingers.'

I gave Adam what I hoped was a withering look. 'Good authority?'

I'd hate to think where he got his information about me. Probably some jealous girl running me down. I get that a lot.

'*You*, actually. You very proudly announced that to me…oh…about two years ago. That night Dodgy Dave's van broke down on the way back from one of those vintage fashion shows you do, and we had to wait hours for the tow truck to turn up.'

Okay, that *did* sound a bit like the sort of thing I'd say when in a particularly full-of-my-own-praises mood, which I might well have been after a successful fashion show. I just hadn't expected Adam to recite it back to me verbatim a whole two years later.

It was true, though. All I had to do was click my crimson-tipped fingers and a whole herd of 'puppies' came running. It was most satisfying.

Sometimes I did it just for the joy of seeing all those eager little faces, not because I actually needed anything.

Adam lounged back on the sofa, resting his head in his hands, his elbows out wide, and gave me a searching look, with a glimmer in his eye that was part amusement, part wariness.

'What?' I asked crossly.

I should have stopped there, not risen to the bait, but I'm far too nosy to do something so virtuous.

I folded my arms across my chest. 'Don't just sit there staring at me!'

'It's all become very clear to me…' he said quietly.

I had the horrible feeling he'd found me out, that he knew exactly what the problem was, but instead of teasing me about it, as I'd have expected him to do, he turned horribly serious. For once, I actually *wanted* him to laugh at me. I wanted him to try to suppress that wicked smile and deliberately drag his answer out, making me tap the heel of my red stiletto impatiently on the floor. But he didn't make me wait at all. Didn't tease me one bit. He just let me have it.

'Yes,' he said, nodding in silent agreement with himself, his expression hardening further. 'You've finally encountered a *puppy* who doesn't want to clamber over the elaborate assault course you've laid out for him.'

CHAPTER TWO

Put Your Head On My Shoulder

Coreen's Confessions

No.2—You'd have thought I'd have got bored with the effect I have on men by now, but I have to say it's still as fun as it ever it was. The day it gets old, I might as well put on a pair of velour jogging bottoms and let myself go.

ADAM stared at the ceiling, his expression still grim. 'Now you know what it's like for the rest of us mere mortals.' And then he started to laugh, shaking his head.

Normally Adam's laugh makes me feel warm inside, but this time it sounded dry and hollow and made me all jittery and bad-tempered. I decided he was just being superior and glared at

him. 'Look, I don't need you to start being all…
avuncular with me—'

He just started laughing again. Properly this time.

'What?' I said, and my voice went all high and scratchy. 'It's a real word!'

I stood up. There was I, practically rigid with tension, and Adam had the audacity to sink even further into the couch, not bothered in the slightest that he was winding me up as far as I would go. I really shouldn't let him do it, but we often start what *seems* to be a normal conversation and before long one of us is seething and the other is chortling. And it doesn't take a massive IQ to work out which one is which.

'You're totally wrong, anyway,' I told him as I sat back down and picked up my fork. I was not going to give him the satisfaction of agreeing with him today.

Anyway, nobody could call Nicholas Chatterton-Jones a *puppy*. He was sleek and dignified, like one of those lean hunting dogs, the ones with silky grey coats and bloodlines going back generations.

I sighed. Just thinking his name made me melt

a little bit. He was the sort of man every girl dreamed of—rich, handsome, debonair. And I was suffering from unrequited *something* for him. Not sure about the 'L' word. That seemed a bit dramatic. But if the symptoms were day-dreaming incessantly about him and looking him up on Google on an hourly basis, I thought I was probably halfway there.

'You're doing it again.'

'What?' I hadn't been doing anything!

But then I realised my ribcage was deflating with the memory of a sigh. I jabbed the captive prawn in Adam's direction. 'Just leave it, will you? It's none of your business.'

I bit the prawn off the fork and glowered at him.

Adam wasn't a puppy either; he was a mongrel. Fully grown. Shaggy and adorable, true, but he'd probably give you fleas if you got close enough.

And he'd hit a nerve with his stupid comment.

Nicholas's sister, Isabella—or Izzi, as she in-sisted being called—was one of the bright young socialites who'd decided that Coreen's Closet was the Next Big Thing, and she shopped here all the time. She'd left university a few years ago and was still trying to decide what she wanted to do next, which left her plenty of time to lunch and party and go to spas while she told her parents she was chewing over her options. Izzi Chatterton-Jones had a heaving social calendar, and she was always needing a new frock for something or other. And now she was sending her friends along to Coreen's Closet too. It was fabulous for business, and Izzi and I had struck up a friendship. Of sorts. We were more than mere acquaintances, but weren't quite at the full-fledged gal pal stage.

But it did mean that Izzi, after being blown away by a vintage cocktail dress I'd found for her in emerald and jet shot silk, had invited me to a couple of her legendary parties, and that was where I'd first clapped eyes on Nicholas.

Just thinking his name caused all the air to leave my body in a breathy rush.

He was tall—well over six foot—had raven-black hair, and cheekbones to make a girl weep. Like a tall Johnny Depp, minus the Cockney pirate accent. No, when Nicholas talked it was all crisp syllables and long words. I could listen to him all day. In the secrecy of my bedroom I'd tried to mimic that tone, that voice, but I'd been born and bred in south London and my vowels just wouldn't do whatever his did to make them so smooth and perfect.

He lived in a different world. One I'd decided I belonged in. Right from an early age I'd always dressed as if I was born for a life of beauty and glamour, and it was high time I stopped merely dreaming about it and acquired the lifestyle to match.

And if I ever *was* going to contemplate a long-term relationship, it couldn't be with just anyone. I needed a man who'd worship me, yes, but some-one who was dashing and exciting too. Someone I could look up to. Someone I wouldn't get bored with. He'd have to be the man of my dreams, in short, and I thought Nicholas was a pretty good candidate.

We'd met on three occasions now. The first couple of times I'd played it cool. I'd glided around the room, looking aloof and elegant, so he could admire me from afar and ask Izzi who that stunning brunette was. Then last weekend I'd decided it was time to make my move.

I heard a crinkling noise and realised Adam had procured the pork balls again without me noticing. I narrowed my eyes at him, but he just sat there, one hand behind his head, smirking at me as he stole the rest of my share.

Hmph. He seemed to have bounced back to his old self annoyingly quickly.

Okay, so maybe there were *two* men in the known universe who weren't inclined to fall at my feet and worship.

But Adam didn't count. I'd known him since I was eight and he was twelve, and his mother had played badminton with my nan. I leaned forward and snatched the paper bag of pork balls from him before he emptied it, ignoring his grunt of displeasure. Then I picked a warm juicy ball of batter out of the bag—the last one!—and dipped it in the accompanying pot of sauce, before sucking a little bit of the bright orange liquid off and biting into it. Adam, however, didn't notice, because he had moved on to the sesame prawn toast.

See? Immune.

My lips are my *second* most frequently stared at body part. They have an almost mesmerising effect on most of the male species. Something I capitalise on, of course. I always paint them red, for maximum visibility and effect. Not that trashy orangey-red. Crimson. The colour of passion and blood. Like the movie queens of old. I'd even seen men dribble watching me eat, and it wasn't the food they'd been gawping at.

But Adam was unimpressed.

Well, maybe not unimpressed. He was my best friend in the whole universe, so that sounded a little harsh. Maybe *unaffected* was a better word. Perhaps it was something to do with the fact that he'd known me before I'd discovered my inner vixen, when I'd been flat-chested, with no waist to speak of. I suppose I ought to have been annoyed about his lack of puppyish adoration, but I wasn't. Although we didn't manage to see each other nowadays as much as we used to he was still my Best Bud. And every girl needs a Best Bud.

He'd been the one to chase away the bullies who'd teased me because I'd lived with my nan growing up. He'd been the one I'd cried on when my favourite boy band had split up, and again when, aged fifteen, I'd cut my own fringe too short by accident. He was the first person I'd phoned the day Alice and I had got the keys to our new shop, and he'd rushed round with a bottle of champagne and all three of us had sat cross-legged on the floor of what would soon be Coreen's Closet and toasted each other with paper cups. Adam was my cheerleader and my big brother and my minder all rolled into one, and I suppose I could forgive him his lack of *puppyishness* for that.

However, thinking about puppies had me dreaming about Nicholas again, and the warm glow I'd generated with my Best Bud thoughts frosted over.

Why didn't he like me? Why?

Last Saturday night had been my latest attempt to catch his eye. I'd gone all out, wearing a strapless red dress that matched my lips and was usually every bit as effective at making men drool. Nicholas had looked straight through me. And when I'd casually joined the group of people he'd been talking to, and had given him my patented eyelash sweep, he hadn't even stuttered. What was wrong with the man?

Normally, just five minutes of concentrated *Coreen* had a bloke eating out of the palm of my hand. I just didn't get it. What was I doing wrong? It was driving me crazy.

I could probably have coped with the blow to my ego if he wasn't *so* gorgeous and *so* blinking perfect. Adam would say it served me right, but that wasn't fair. Nobody deserved to be this miserable. And I'd felt this way for *three* whole weeks now. If something didn't happen to change Nicholas's mind soon, I'd be ready for those velour jogging bottoms after all!

'So...'

Adam leaned forward and offered me a conciliatory prawn toast from the foil container he'd had resting on his knee, catching my gaze with his. I ignored the prawn toast and concentrated on those warm brown eyes.

'Who's this paragon of manliness that's got you all tied up in knots?

I recognised the way Adam was looking at me. He was trying to appear all relaxed and jokey, but there was a glint of seriousness at the back of his eyes. Probably worried about me. That was the minder-slash-big-brother side of him coming out. But maybe that was a good thing. Adam's shoulders, while possibly not as broad and honed as Nicholas's, were perfect for crying on.

The only problem was, at present Adam didn't

look much as if he wanted to mop up my tears with his shirt. His expression was guarded again, and his flinty eyes felt as if they were boring holes into my forehead. I didn't have any sassy comebacks left; my store of outrageous comments was worryingly empty. So I just looked back at him with blinking eyes, as close to begging as I ever came.

Adam's eyes didn't exactly soften and melt, but he stood up and rubbed my arm. 'He's an idiot, whoever he is,' he said gruffly.

Then he took my hand and led me to the sofa. He even let me sit on the side where the springs weren't so dodgy. Once I had arranged my skirt and petticoat carefully, he dropped onto the other side and looked at me.

I sighed, and it was long and heartfelt. There was no point trying to hide it now. 'The idiot in question is Nicholas Chatterton-Jones. He's the brother of one of my best customers.'

Adam frowned. 'Chatterton-Jones? Isn't he...? Doesn't he own that investment company? Eagle something or other?'

'That's him.' I could feel myself sinking even deeper into the sofa, but it wasn't a relaxing kind of feeling. It was as if all the energy was leaching right out of me.

He whistled. 'He's the one that almost played rugby for England, but an injury stopped him.'

I just wilted a little further, my head bobbing in agreement. I knew every date and event of Nicholas's personal history, and quite a lot about the previous three generations of the Chatterton-Jones family. Sometimes an internet connection can be a girl's worst enemy.

I looked at Adam and took a deep breath. We both knew the game we were about to play. We always did this for each other when one of us was down. Friend A would relay the issue of contention, while Friend B nodded in all the right places and supplied suitably supportive comments, even if those comments were either a) outrageously optimistic or b) patent falsehoods.

'He's just not attracted to me in the slightest,' I said mournfully.

Adam shook his head. 'What? The guy must be blind!' He was grinning as he said this, and the cold feeling that had been churning my stomach began to disappear. The truth was that Adam was much better at being Friend B than I was.

He always knew exactly the right thing to say to cheer me up, and he always said it with that slightly devilish look in his eye—a sure-fire way to get me to smile. But behind the cheeky look I knew he was also a little bit serious, that despite the jovial nature of our banter he believed in me.

Told you he was my Best Bud.

'It gets worse,' I added, almost starting to enjoy moaning about my spectacular flirting flop of the previous Saturday. 'I made a complete fool of myself.'

'Now, I find that very hard to believe.' The sarcastic sparkle in Adam's eyes made me want to hit him. It also made me want to laugh.

We carried on like that for quite some time. Me relaying a blow-by-blow account of the party and Adam commiserating and commenting with precision and great comic timing. Only the momentary lift from Adam's sideswipes didn't improve my mood this time. The more I talked, the more morose I felt. Even Adam seemed to wince slightly with each mortifying detail, and I could tell he was struggling to keep his Friend B smile in place. We both fell quiet, knowing that we were losing our game, not sure that carrying on would salvage anything.

He gave me a softer, less Adam-like smile, and I leaned across and rested my head on his shoulder. It really was a lovely shoulder. Warm. Comforting. Solid. I wanted to believe things were going to work out right, but in my heart of hearts I just wasn't sure. It might sound big-headed, but being invisible to a man was a new experience for me. I didn't like the way it brought back flickers of other memories of being passed over, being invisible. Old memories, ones I'd done everything in my power to erase.

'What am I doing wrong?' I whispered. Adam was a man. I know he wasn't the same type of guy as Nicholas, but he had to have some kind of insight. They must have more in common than just shared biology.

That was it! That was the thing both Adam and Nicholas had in common.

I sat up and looked at Adam. 'Why don't *you* find me attractive?'

If I could work that one out, maybe I could find a way to reach Nicholas after all.

Adam looked stunned. I suppose it wasn't that

surprising. We didn't ever really talk about the fact that he was a boy and I was a girl. I knew he'd rather veer away from this topic of conversation, but I batted my lashes and gave him a look that said *Please*…

He chewed the inside of his mouth for a few moments. 'I've never said I don't find you attractive, Coreen. A guy would have to be *unconscious* not to find you attractive.'

Well, now it was my turn to be stunned.

Adam gave a one-shouldered shrug. His lazy demeanour had returned and he didn't look at all bothered by what he'd just said.

'Then why haven't you…? Why have we never…?'

'Hooked up?' he suggested.

I pulled a face. That sounded kind of tacky. Adam wasn't the sort of guy you 'hooked up' with. He was keeper material. And I didn't like the thought of anyone treating him in such a… *disposable* manner.

'See? That face you just made is one of many reasons why.'

I shook my head. He was taking it all the wrong way. The face I'd pulled didn't mean—

'And I've seen the way you treat men, remember? I've never jumped through hoops for you and I never will.'

I gasped. There had never been any hoops! Well…not for Adam.

He read my mind and fixed me with a knowing stare. 'How did it go? Oh, yes. I remember…' He did a rather good impression of my eyelash sweep and added an earthy, softer tone to his voice. If I hadn't been so horrified I might have admitted it sounded quite a lot like me. "Adam, sweetie, would you mind coming along with me to a party this evening? I know it's short notice, but I could really do with some moral support."'

And then he flicked some pretend hair away from his shoulder, and I forgot to be horrified and descended into giggles. Adam, strangely enough, wasn't laughing so hard.

'When we got to said party I realised my role was more *stooge* than *moral support*.'

I stopped laughing. 'That's not true!'

He raised his eyebrows at me.

I opened my mouth to protest, but thought better of it. I'd buried that memory—along with a whole host of others from those days—quite

effectively until that moment. It all came back
to me with searing clarity: Adam's face, his jaw
set. The way he'd stormed from the party. They
weren't moments in my life I wanted to be reminded of.

I bit my lip. Something I hoped would show my
contrition. Although—and I honestly did out of
sheer habit this time—I knew it made me look
very appealing too.

'That was a long time ago. Back when we were
teenagers. Teenagers do lots of stupid things.'

'Like kissing their best friend in front of the
whole room when the current Romeo is being a
slightly harder nut to crack?'

Oh, hell. I'd actually done that too, hadn't I?
Not that I'd planned it, though. I'd just got carried
away in the heat of the moment.

Adam hadn't spoken to me for a month after
Sharon's party, even though I'd wheedled and
whined and pulled every trick in the book to get
him to forgive me. In the end I'd just turned up on
his doorstep one day—no tricks up my sleeve, not
even any make-up on—and begged him to give
me another chance, to say we could be friends
again. There'd been a huge Adam-shaped hole in

my life. One I hadn't cared for very much. One I hadn't thought I could go on living with. Its presence had nibbled away at my very soul.

Adam had forgiven me. Eventually. But since then we'd both tacitly agreed to ignore the boy-girl element to our relationship, and I must have done a pretty good job of it if I'd managed to forget how atrociously I'd behaved.

'I'm sorry,' I said quietly. 'I'm such a horrible person. No wonder Nicholas Chatterton-Jones wants nothing to do with me.' And this time I wasn't even angling for a compliment. I really meant it.

Adam pulled me close again and let out a long breath. 'Don't be silly. You're fabulous. You know you are. It's just that I realised that you won't let the men in your life be anything *but* "puppies", and I'm the sort that refuses to wear a collar and lead for anyone—not even you. So for that reason, and probably a few more, I decided we work better as friends.' And then he kissed the top of my head.

One corner of my mouth tried to smile.

Adam carried on talking, and I could feel his warm breath in my hair. 'I have to warn you…

well…I'm sorry to say I don't think you stand a chance with this one. You'd better find yourself a different puppy to train.'

Sorry? He didn't sound sorry in the slightest.

I sat up and looked at him sharply. 'What do you mean?'

He hesitated, and I half hoped he would drop it. Adam and I didn't have conversations like this. But then, instead of looking down at his battered old trainers, he looked me straight in the eye. I held my breath. Just a little.

'Guys like Chatterton-Whatsit… Well, some-time *less is more*. That's all I'm saying.'

'You think I'm too…?' I trailed off, not quite sure how to label myself.

'Maybe.'

I frowned. 'But that's who I am! Nicholas Chatterton-Jones might be a god, but I'm not changing myself for anybody.'

Adam looked rather weary. He shook his head. 'That's not what I'm saying. It's just that there's a girl underneath all of—' he waved his hand to encompass the hairspray, the lipstick, the polka dots '—*this*. Just don't forget that.'

I didn't know what to say to that. Of course I

brushed the hairspray out and took the lipstick off at night. I knew what I looked like without all of it. It was just that all of *this*, as Adam had so articulately put it, was how I felt on the inside. I only dressed the outside up to match.

I scowled at him. It felt as if he was criticising me, and I didn't care for it much.

'What makes you such an expert at relationships?' I said sulkily, folding my arms and shifting back to rest against the opposite end of the sofa. 'You haven't had a serious girlfriend since Hannah, and that was a good couple of years ago.'

Adam matched my position, folding his arms across his shirt. 'I've been working hard on building the business up. I haven't had time for relationships. Unlike some people I know, I don't think it's fair to toy with people and then drop them when it suits me.'

See? This was why we should have never veered into to this territory. It was all getting horribly messy, and the lovely, smiling, joking Adam I knew had totally disappeared. I suspected that I too was being less than my normal charming self, but I wasn't about to back down, and I wasn't about to let my Best Bud analyse me further.

'You never did tell me why it all fizzled out with Hannah. Did she get fed up with you spending all your time mucking about in garden sheds?'

That was below the belt, I knew. But Adam's role was to make me feel better, not kick me when I was down, so he'd kind of brought it on himself.

He looked away. 'My heart just wasn't in it. I wanted it to be, but it wasn't. And it wasn't fair to Hannah to keep pretending.'

Blast, Adam! Just when I was all revved up for a cat fight, he had to go and get all honest on me and deflate my nice little bubble of adrenaline.

He looked back at me, an expression in his eyes I hadn't seen many times before. 'I hate it when you get like this about my job. I'm proud of what I've achieved, and I've been nothing but supportive of you.'

Urgh. I felt like an utter heel. He was right. I was taking cheap shots at my best friend just because some guy had had the nerve not to fall instantly at my feet. I was behaving despicably.

'I'm sorry,' I said. I would have gone on, but

there was a lump as big as one of my paste brooches in my throat.

Adam put his hand on top of mine and squeezed. 'Apology accepted. You've really got it bad for this Nicholas guy, haven't you?'

. He looked slightly pained, as if he was sharing my misery. I nodded, and my whole insides started to ache. I don't normally do the crying thing. Who has the time when liquid liner and three coats of mascara are involved? But I'd got this stinging sensation right up at the top of my nose and I knew I was perilously close.

I didn't know why I liked Nicholas so much. Apart from the obvious looks-like-a-Greek-god, has-piles-of-cash thing. It was more than that. I never usually let guys get to me this way. Adam was right. Normally I *was* the one pulling all the strings. But there was something about Nicholas that had called out to me right from the start. I had a feeling he might be the elusive cupcake that would assuage my nagging hunger and satisfy all my sweet-toothed desires.

The stinging got worse. I looked at my shoes. Beautiful red peep-toe creations. But even they made me sad, and I didn't even really know why.

Maybe Nan was right. Maybe something *was* ticking inside me. I was almost thirty, after all. But, seeing as I was…well, *me,* I was obviously going for the full-fledged meltdown rather than the polite *tick-tock* in the background of my life. Nan always says I can't do anything unless I make a production out of it.

Adam shuffled closer on the sofa, so his arm was touching mine. He leaned down to try and see into my eyes, and nudged me. 'Coreen…?'

My bottom lip slid forward. 'Maybe you're right. Maybe I am too *much* for Nicholas Chatterton-Jones.' I shrugged and tipped my head slightly to look at him. 'It's a moot point now, anyway. I found out a couple of days ago that Nicholas might be off the market soon. There are rumours about a possible new girlfriend.'

Adam gave me a lopsided smile. 'That's never stopped you before.'

I punched him on the arm. 'That makes me sound awful! I've never actually stolen a man away from anyone. I can't help it if they take one look at me and realise I'm the one they can't live without.'

Adam pressed his lips together and nodded

sagely. 'That's what I love about you—your matchless modesty.'

I punched him again. And then I smiled. How did he do that?

He put up his fists and nudged me on the shoulder with one of them. 'So? Who's this girlfriend? Do you think you can take her?'

I swatted his hand away, but he kept jabbing me gently on the upper arm, the way boxers did when they warmed up with one of those swinging punch bags.

'I'm going to take *you* down in a minute, if you don't cut that out!' I said, laughing.

The devilish twinkle was back. 'Promises, promises,' he said.

'It's that awful Louisa Fanshawe,' I said, not rising to the bait. And if we were talking fisticuffs, I probably *could* take her. She was another one of those willowy sorts who'd blow away in a stiff breeze. I wouldn't risk breaking a nail on her, though, so she was safe on that count.

'Oh, yes. I've heard how awful she is,' Adam replied. 'All that charity work…visiting sick children in hospital and campaigning for the homeless. It's positively disgusting.'

I jabbed him in the ribs with my elbow. He was supposed to be on my side, so why was he practically bouncing up and down? What had he to be so happy about? I decided to direct my ire at the absent Louisa.

'When she's not swanning up and down a catwalk for some pretentious designer,' I pointed out.

I thought about Louisa Fanshawe and her stick-like limbs and big doleful eyes. She wasn't exactly pretty, but I'd allow for the fact she was striking—in that understated, slightly duck-faced way some high fashion models were. The women on Nicholas's arm always looked frighteningly similar. Duck-faced and stick-thin was obviously his type.

I sighed again. Louisa was the *less* Adam had been talking about. I looked down at my chest. *Less* wasn't something I had a lot of. I was doomed.

I was about to point this out to Adam, but when I looked up at him he was paying an inordinate amount of attention to the last of the prawn toasts. I think he felt me looking at him, because he offered me the foil tray. I shook my head. 'You have it.'

He demolished it in one bite, and then turned to look me straight in the eyes. 'Like I said…' The seriousness there made my pulse kick. 'The guy's an idiot.'

I felt a smile start somewhere deep in my chest and work its way up to my mouth. 'I love you, Best Bud,' I said, and wrapped my arms around his neck and pulled him close.

For a long time he was silent and he just held me, soothing me with the rhythmic warmth of his breath on my neck. Then the inhaling and exhaling stopped. Seconds and seconds seemed to drag past before it started again, and when the next breath came there were words floating on it.

'It's hard not to,' he whispered into my neck.

And then I hit him again.

CHAPTER THREE

The Very Thought of You

Coreen's Confessions
No.3—You'd think that someone as vain
as I am would enjoy looking in the mirror,
but sometimes I just can't face it.

I CONTINUED to mope around for the next few days, and the more I thought about it, the more I thought that maybe Nan was right about something ticking inside me.

Of course I didn't tell Nan that I might be on the verge of getting serious with someone when I visited her the following Sunday. She'd have had me up at the church to book a date so fast my head would've spun. Baby steps. Just thinking about being with one man for a considerable chunk of time was about as far as I wanted to go at present.

No, when I visited Nan we did what we always did—ate roast dinner, drank tea, and planed to watch an old black-and-white movie on the telly. After lunch I observed a further ritual. I went into the spare bedroom, opened the rickety wardrobe, and looked at all the dresses hanging there in their clear plastic covers.

They had been my mother's. She'd died about ten years earlier, in a shabby little bed and breakfast in Blackpool, killed silently, invisibly and senselessly by a faulty boiler spurting carbon monoxide. And when she hadn't turned up to go on stage that night at the club they'd just slotted another singer into the bill and carried on. It shouldn't be that easy to replace someone, should it? People ought be remembered for their unique qualities, even if the choices they made in life weren't ones you respected, or even understood.

As I did most weeks, I pulled out just one of Mum's stage dresses and studied it more closely. This one was all shoulder pads and sequins, probably from around the time she'd met my dad. I could imagine Mum, her big Joan Collins-style hair stiff with half a can of hairspray, singing a soft rock ballad into a microphone, her eyes closed and her heart on her sleeve. She'd had a lovely voice. I had a few cassette tapes at home, but I didn't play them much—too scared they'd warp or wear out.

Her voice had been rich and husky, able to catch every nuance of emotion in a song, whether she was belting it out or making the audience hang on every note. By rights she should have had more success than she did. And maybe she would have done if she'd put all the energy she'd wasted trailing round the country after my father into her career instead.

Despite my love of vintage, I never tried on these clothes. The eighties weren't my thing, for a start. I knew the dresses would probably fit, but I didn't want to look in the mirror and see my mother staring back at me. I didn't want to see that same broken hopelessness in my eyes.

'Go on—take them down to that shop of yours and get a few quid for them,' Nan said from behind me.

I hadn't heard her come in the room. I shook my head, carefully put the dress in its place on the rail and shut the wardrobe door. Nan gave me a sympathetic smile.

'Cuppa? And that Dirk Bogarde film starts in a few minutes.'

I shook off the sadness that had collected like dust on my mother's abandoned clothes and smiled back. 'That would be perfect.'

I loved my Nan. I'd never seen her feathers ruffled, and for someone who'd produced two generations of drama queens she was as sensible and grounded as they came. I hadn't minded living with her when I was a kid. There had always been cake and cuddles at Nan's little terraced house. And Nan made everything seem warm and cosy. She never got that far-off look in her eyes that made you feel as if she was thinking of someone else, wanting to be somewhere else, while you tried to tell her about the gold star you'd got for your school project.

It had been easy to fall into the trap of believing I lived with Nan because Mum was always up and down the country, singing in clubs and pubs, or off on cruise ships. While there was a certain amount of truth in that, after her death I'd started to see another reason for her not giving up the club circuit and settling down. Leaving that life behind would have meant giving up hope—

hope that she'd bump into Dad, hope that he'd fall in love with her all over again and come home. While she sat in a never-ending succession of grubby backstage changing rooms, putting her false eyelashes and sequins on, she could still deny the truth, pretend that day still might come, when really the dream had expired many years before.

But I didn't like to think of Mum like that, sad and alone, pining for a man who would never love her the way she had loved him. I liked to remember the happy times. Like when she came home and stayed in the spare room at Nan's. When I was really small I used to come over all shy at first. I'd be awed by the glamorous lady sitting on Nan's old-fashioned brown sofa. But it hadn't taken me long to get all loud and demanding, to be clambering all over her and tugging her to my bedroom to see my toys. I even used to make her hold my hand while I went to sleep.

My favourite memories of her were the times she'd let me dress up in her clothes. She'd even backcomb my hair and put silvery eyeshadow on me. And then I'd clump around the spare bedroom in her shoes, singing one of her songs, doing all the actions, and she'd fall back on the bed and laugh until she cried. My mum had a lovely laugh.

'Custard Cream?'

I looked up to see Nan offering me a battered tartan tin that, back in 1973, had once contained Christmas shortbread. I'd been so lost in my memories that I'd followed her into the living room and sat down in an armchair on automatic. The titles of the film were staring to roll, so I nabbed a couple of biscuits, balanced them on the arm of the chair, and prepared myself to slip into a world where men were noble, women had impossible eyebrows, and violins expressed every emotion while the actors stayed stiff-lipped, clenching their fists. I quite liked the idea of standing motionless at a moment of crisis, all elegant and dramatic, while an orchestra swelled around me.

I looked down at my floral Capri pants and red suede ballet pumps. Not sure I'd like to live in black and white, though. I'm a Technicolor kind of gal, I suppose.

We were ten minutes into the film when my mobile rang. Nan tutted, but didn't swerve her gaze from Dirk, looking all square-jawed and beautiful on the screen, so I picked up my cup of tea and walked into the kitchen to answer it.

'Oh, *God*, sweetie! I'm *so* relieved it didn't go to voicemail!'

I'd recognise those upper-class tones anywhere. Unlike her brother, whose rich voice was even and restrained, Izzi Chatterton-Jones had a dramatic delivery that made booking a table at her favourite restaurant sound as if it was a life-and-death event. If Izzi had been a character in a novel, her dialogue would have been riddled with italics.

'Hi, Izzi. What can—?'

'I've had the most *fabulous* idea, darling, and you've simply *got* to help me with it.'

Knowing Izzi, whatever she was planning would be probably be last minute and extremely stressful to say yes to. On the other hand she was bags of fun, and I might even get to see Nicholas again.

'I'm going to host a country house party!' Izzi squealed. 'Mummy and Daddy are going to the South of France for the whole of July, and they've said I can borrow the house for an entire week-end. Isn't that the most *super* idea ever?'

She paused, probably waiting for me to recover from swooning with excitement. Only I wasn't. I couldn't think of anything worse—mud, rain, horsey laughs, everyone dressed in drab tweeds and shooting anything that twitched? Count me out. I was eternally grateful that Nicholas seemed to spend most of his time in London, in his tall white house with black railings in Belgravia. Now, I wouldn't object to spending a weekend *there*, given half the chance.

'Well, what do you think?' Izzi asked, a hint of impatience in her tone.

'Super,' I said, borrowing her vocabulary. None of the words I had in mind would have gone down well. 'But what's this got to do with me?'

'It's a murder-mystery weekend!'

Okay. I know that compared to the Chatterton-Joneses I'm merely a commoner, but did I really look like the kind of girl who knew how to do someone in? It must be the accent. Although mine was a lot softer than true Cockney, Izzi and her sort probably thought I knew the East End like the back of my hand and was distantly related to the Krays or descended from Jack the Ripper.

'I…er…don't think I've ever been on one of those,' I said. 'What's involved?'

'I want to do the whole caboodle—costumes and everything—and that's where you come in!'

Oh, goody.

'I can't abide those fancy dress shop monstrosities,' she added airily.

I stifled a giggle. The thought of Izzi in a padded Superman outfit, complete with six-pack and biceps, had sprung to my mind, and it made it very hard to listen properly.

'…so if you can sort all of that out it would be fabulous.'

Huh? Oh, dear. I'd wandered off again. Thankfully I have a full range of phrases tucked away at the back of my head for such eventualities. Sounding very serious, I said, 'Could you be more specific?'

Izzi launched into a long spiel about wanting authentic thirties clothes for her Agatha Christie-type murder-mystery weekend, and I swear if I had been a cartoon my eyeballs would have been spinning round in my head and dinging like cash registers. Daywear, eveningwear and accessories for eight people! And Izzi only likes the very best stuff. I didn't care that I was missing Dirk smouldering on Nan's ancient telly for this. If things went well in the next year or two I was thinking of opening another branch of Coreen's Closet, somewhere closer to the West End, and Izzi's connections would really speed things along.

'It's going to be such a hoot!' Izzi said. 'We've all got characters to play. I'll e-mail you details of every part so you can start hunting for suitable clothes.'

'What's your budget?'

Izzi made a dismissive noise, as I'd suspected she would. 'I care more about it being *right* than I do about the cost,' she said, and then she giggled. 'I have the most fabulous part for you!'

I raised my eyebrows. I'd been hoping she'd say I was on the guest list, but hadn't wanted to assume. This could have just been a business transaction, after all. I grinned to myself.

Izzi started telling me about the different characters the organisers she'd hired had outlined to her—lords, ladies, parlour maids and debutantes. And then she started reeling off the guest list.

When she said Nicholas's name my heart started to skip.

'I can't wait,' I said softly. I wasn't just being excited for Izzi's benefit now. I really meant it. This was my opportunity! I'd be able to relax and mingle with Nicholas outside of a hot, crowded cocktail party. I'd be able to dial things down a bit—just as Adam had suggested—and Nicholas would be able to see my relaxed, fun side. I could see it all so clearly: languid cocktails in the drawing room before dinner, fresh, misty country mornings…

Izzi developed a stern edge to her voice. 'And I need you to bring a man!'

I'd been deep in a fantasy where Nicholas and I had been strolling though a secluded bluebell wood. I had stepped in a rabbit hole and twisted my ankle, and he'd swept me into his arms and carried me back to the house as if I weighed nothing. (This was a fantasy, after all.) I could almost smell his woody aftershave as I laid my head against his chest…

'What?' I said, a little too sharply.

'It's a dealbreaker if you can't,' Izzi said. 'I'm *desperate*! Jonti broke his leg bungee jumping,

and is stuck in New Zealand, and Jonathan refuses to miss some horrible cricket match. You've
got to bring someone!'

The bluebells, the rabbit hole, the lovely feeling of being safe in Nicholas's arms? They all
disappeared into that mist I'd been daydreaming
about. I was glad Izzi couldn't see me, because
I felt my eyebrows clench together and my jaw
tense.

The last thing I wanted to do was bring a date
on Izzi's weekend! It would spoil everything.
While Adam had pointed out that I hadn't been
above being seen with another man to spark a potential conquest's interest in the past, I'd learned
my lesson on that front, and I'd never get any
time alone with Nicholas if I had a *lovelorn swain*
lolloping around after me all weekend. Also, I
didn't want to encourage any of them needlessly.
The only man I was interested in at the moment
was Nicholas, and it wasn't fair to give any other
impression.

What was it that Adam had said about toying
with people the other night? Hmm. I decided I
must be maturing.

'It's a bit short notice,' I muttered to Izzi, but she just laughed.

'I can't believe you haven't got a hundred men ready to fall over themselves for a weekend with you. You'll manage it somehow.'

I pouted. Sometimes having a reputation like mine was not a good thing. Not that I'm a floozy. I might get a lot of male attention—I might even enjoy it—but I do *try* not to encourage it unless I'm interested. And I'm actually quite picky about who I go out with. There have been far fewer men in my life than most people think.

Flip. What was I going to do? I really needed this weekend to be a success for me—in more ways than one. I supposed I could fob Izzi off, hoping she was just blowing hot air about it being a deal breaker, but what if she stood her ground if I called her bluff? And she just might. One of the reasons I liked Izzi was that she was unpredictable and prone to sudden whims, just like me. If I caught her in the wrong mood when I let it slip I would be coming alone, she might just pull the plug on me. It's the sort of thing I might have done in her place.

And then an idea struck me. Beautiful in its

simplicity—except for the fact the man in question would never go for it. But Izzi was right: I'd
manage it somehow.

'Don't worry,' I said cheerily. 'I have the perfect
guy in mind.'

'Why do I have the horrible feeling there's a catch
involved?' Adam asked me from the other end of
the rowing boat. I couldn't see him properly. We
were under tall sycamores on one corner of the
boating pond and I couldn't make out his features
because the aggressive June sun was behind him,
causing me to squint. However, even though he
was just one big, soft blur, I knew there was a
twinkle in his eyes.

Adam's twinkle is a really good sign. It usually means he *wants* to say yes to whatever I'm
trying to get him to agree to, but is just having
fun with me in the meantime.

I adjusted my parasol. 'Why would there have
to be a catch?' I said sweetly.

'Oh, I dunno…' The oars swept out of the water
and propelled us forward in an exhilarating little
jerk. 'Maybe because you invited me out for an
afternoon stroll in Greenwich Park—rest and

relaxation, you said—and I end up doing all the work while you sit there licking an ice cream cone.'

'I said I'd get you one when our time is up,' I replied. I couldn't see what he was fussing about. A little bit of delayed gratification is good for the soul.

The oars hit the water again, and I couldn't help noticing the fine hairs on Adam's forearms as we emerged into the sunshine again. Hairs that shifted and shimmered as the muscles underneath them bunched and relaxed. There's something very captivating about watching a man row. I'd have to make sure that I ended up in a boat with Nicholas at some point during the country weekend. There must be a lake somewhere on the Chatterton-Joneses' estate. It's that kind of place.

I decided to get in some practice and attempted to drape myself fetchingly at my end of the boat, doing my best to look elegant and ethereal.

'Now you're just rubbing it in,' Adam muttered.

I closed my eyes and smiled, my face turned up to the sun. The twinkle was still there. I could *hear* it.

'All I'm asking for is one lick,' he said softly, and I belatedly realised we were drifting rather than see-sawing through the water. I opened my eyes to find Adam much closer than I'd thought he'd be. The twinkle was there, all right, but there was something behind it, something hot and bright. That aggressive sun reflected in them, perhaps. I shifted my parasol. I must have let it slip back when I'd had my eyes closed, because I could feel my cheeks heating now.

For some reason I couldn't find the words to refuse. He leaned closer and closer, a lazy smile spreading across his face. The chocolate in those eyes began to melt. I couldn't help but watch it swirl and warm, filling my vision until it was almost the only thing I saw. It was odd, because we were hardly moving it all, yet it was at that moment I felt a quiver of seasickness in my tummy.

Just as he was close enough to lick my ice cream, as we were cocooned under my parasol and it seemed we were the only two beings in the whole of Greenwich Park, I felt a tug on my fingers and the cone was eased from my hand. There was a sudden lurch and a splash, and I found myself sitting alone in the rowing boat while Adam waded through the knee-deep water to the edge of the stone-lined pond, eating my ice cream in big gulps and laughing as he went.

I was so surprised I nearly dropped my parasol. And then Adam really would have been in big trouble. It was made of exquisite cream lace, and I hadn't seen another one to rival it in years. I caught it just in time, and snapped it closed. Then, still listening to the sound of Adam chuckling from the safety of dry land, I swapped seats and picked up the oars.

I'll bet you thought I couldn't row. Well, I can. I'm rather good at it, actually. Boating ponds were cheap entertainment when I was a kid, and Nan and I used to come here all the time when it was sunny.

It was just as well I was facing away from Adam, because I was seething under my breath. The sight of me rowing expertly towards him just made him laugh harder, for some reason. I wanted to kill him.

Only I couldn't. I needed him to do me a favour, didn't I? A pretty big one. And if that meant sucking up my pride so I could further my business and snaffle the man of my dreams, so be it. I could be the bigger person while Adam continued to act like a kid. I could.

I reached the stone lip of the boating pond and marshalled my features to show none of my irritation. By the time I'd neatly nipped out of the boat—blowing a kiss at the scruffy teenager in charge of the pond so he'd come and fetch it instead of making me row it to the proper place—I was the pinnacle of elegant calm. I had a picture of Grace Kelly in my head, and I was determined not to lose it.

I caught up with Adam at the ice cream van, where he handed me a replacement cone, complete with chocolate flake and strawberry sauce. I snatched it from him and walked away.

'Now you owe me,' I said. To his credit, he didn't disagree. Well, not straight away. We both walked, giving our attention to our ice creams until we were halfway up the hill.

'I don't think half an ice cream really equates to a whole weekend in the country dressed up like a wally.'

He might have a point there, but I was hardly going to acknowledge that, was I? 'These are *very* good ice creams,' I said, as I pushed the last of mine into my cone with my tongue. Adam went quiet. I looked up to find him swallowing. Hard. He had a strange look on his face, and I had a horrible feeling he was about to say something I wouldn't like, so I started off up the hill again.

He caught up to me fairly quickly. 'Come and see my latest project and we'll call it quits,' he said.

I sighed. 'I've visited everything you've constructed for years.'

He shook his head. 'Not for quite some time, actually. You'd be surprised at what I'm doing now.'

I wasn't convinced. A summerhouse was a summerhouse, and a shed was a shed, after all. Not that I'm not proud of him for turning his hobby into a business that keeps him afloat, but it's hardly glamorous. Wherever you find wood like that, there are inevitably spiders. And I'm not big on spiders.

'And this thing you've being doing down in Kent is wildly different, is it?'

'I finished that months ago. I was talking about the hotel project in Malaysia.'

I almost choked on the last of my cornet. 'I can't afford the airfare for somewhere like that! I need all my spare cash for Coreen's Closet.'

There was a hard edge in Adam's voice when he replied. 'I wasn't asking you to pay,' he said. 'I was asking you to come.' He picked up speed, and I had to scurry after him in my crimson slingbacks. I tugged at his shirtsleeve.

'Okay, I'll come,' I said, at once trying to work out how I could talk myself out of flying thousands of miles to look at a few treehouses in the jungle without *actually* breaking my word. I don't like jungles. At least I don't imagine I would. The nearest I've been to jungle is the palm house in Kew Gardens, but I got all hot and sticky and my hair started to frizz. Don't care to repeat the experience unless I really have to.

Adam stopped walking and gave me a long, searching look. I tried not to squirm. He knew I would try and wriggle out of it, and I knew that he knew. And he knew that I knew that he knew. It was all very tiring. And embarrassing.

I don't like letting Adam down, but seriously… a trip to a frizz-inducing jungle in exchange for a weekend at an idyllic country estate? Now who was being unfair?

Adam started walking again. This time his steps were slow and measured.

'Even if I come, I'm not going to help you snag this Nicholas Chatterton-Jones. I'm not sure I like the sound of him.'

I huffed. There he was, going all big-brotherish on me again. But I supposed I could put up with a bit of sibling protectiveness if it meant I got what I wanted.

I lifted my chin. 'I don't need you to help me,' I said airily. That part I could do all by myself. 'I need you to help keep Izzi sweet. It's a good business opportunity, and I need this to be a success. If Izzi decides I'm out of favour, I might as well kiss my expansion plans goodbye. She has a very wide circle of influence, and I want that influence working on my behalf, not against me.'

Adam nodded. 'Why me? Why not one of the puppies?'

I rolled my eyes. 'Because you have the uncanny knack of getting on with everyone and fitting in anywhere, and I need someone who *knows*, not just thinks, that I'm fabulous.'

And there it was again. The laugh. Why couldn't this man ever take me seriously?

I cleared my throat and gave him a superior look. 'Will you do it?'

He turned to look down the hill over the Thames to the odd mix of elegant Georgian buildings and silvery skyscrapers. 'I'll think about it,' he said.

CHAPTER FOUR

These Foolish Things

**Coreen's Confessions
No.4—I only ever wear red shoes. It started off as a coincidence, but then became a choice. Now it's a divine ordinance.**

A WEEK later I found myself standing in a leafy square in Belgravia, outside a tall white house. I took in a breath and held it. I'd e-mailed Adam six times, with *gentle* little messages asking if he'd meet me here, and whether he'd decided to come to the murder-mystery weekend in a fortnight's time, but I hadn't got a reply as yet.

He *had* sent me a link to an online video showing a yappy little dog worrying the life out of a bone, though. I didn't get why. Sometimes Adam's sense of humour can be a little…strange.

Anyway, if Adam wasn't going to come, I was

going to have to do this all by myself. No problem. Nan always says that a sense of style and good manners will help a girl fit in anywhere. Okay, Nan only really mentions the good manners, but the rest *feels* true. I turned my attention back to the house.

The Chatterton-Joneses had made their money in the early nineteenth century, bringing silks back from India, although none of them worked in the importing business these days. Nicholas could have decided to rest on the well-padded family laurels, but he was the successful and intuitive head of an investment group, wealthy in his own right.

I looked at the large sash windows, the freshly painted black wrought-iron railings, and swallowed. I'd spent most of my life living in Nan's tiny terraced house in Catford, the whole floor space of which could probably fit into the entrance hall of this quietly elegant home. No time for nerves, though. I was here to perform a function, and it was time to show Nicholas just how slick and sophisticated I could be.

'Darling, what *are* you doing standing in the street? I almost took you for a stalker.'

I turned to see Izzi coming to a halt beside me, looking effortlessly classy in a cream trouser suit and matching coat. Large sunglasses covered half her face, protecting it from the bright summer morning. Now that Izzi had arrived, the riot of petunias that I'd been admiring only moments before in the square seemed a little brash.

I'd aimed for 'classy' myself, but I was suddenly aware that my dark grey suit, made more than fifty years ago by a competent home seamstress copying a Lilli Ann design, wasn't quite in the same league. And it wasn't just clothing that separated us. She exuded the kind of casual elegance that only generations of confidence could breed, whereas I was more a combination of Nan's Blitz Spirit, my mother's need for drama, and something that a clipped-voiced character in a black-and-white film would call 'pluck'.

But it was all I had to fall back on, so I was just going to have to make it work for me.

Izzi linked her arm through mine and swept me up the short flight of steps towards Nicholas's glossy black door. 'I'm sorry my brother is being pig-headed about getting himself measured for his outfits, and for dragging you all the way over here on your day off to give us all a fitting, but I want this weekend to be a success, and with only a fortnight left I don't have time to deal with his tantrums.'

I smiled gently. No one in their right mind could ever imagine Nicholas Chatterton-Jones having a tantrum! He was far too inscrutable for that. Snarling like a panther, maybe…

'I've texted him three times!' Izzi was saying. 'He just keeps saying he's too busy to mess around with tape measures, so here you are! If the mountain won't come to Mohammed… The rest of the gang should be here within the next half-hour, but I thought you'd like to get Nicky done first.'

I suddenly got a sinking feeling—as if I'd swallowed Nicholas's big lion-head brass knocker and it was now settling in my stomach. Nicholas did know I was coming, didn't he? But before I'd had a chance to check Izzi hadn't sprung a trap on him she'd rapped the ring the lion held in its mouth against the door and turned to me.

'You do have your tape measure, don't you?'

I was far too nervous about what was happening behind that big black door to do anything but reach into my alligator handbag and produce it with a flourish.

Now, I knew some people didn't like the idea of me carrying real reptile skin around with me, but be fair! I'd had nothing to do with the unfortunate beast's demise, and the very least a kind soul could do after all it had been through was show it a little love and tenderness, and I certainly gave it plenty of that.

Besides, it matched my burgundy heels perfectly.

Just as the door creaked open I heard footsteps behind me, pounding down the pavement, and I turned to see a rather out-of-breath Adam darting up the steps to Nicholas's front door. He gave me a quick grin and fell into step behind us as we entered the cool and silent hallway. Once inside, Izzi peeled off her glasses and turned to look at Adam.

'So you're the man Coreen found,' she said loftily.

I started to glare at her. Just because Adam builds sheds and treehouses for a living, it doesn't mean that he's not in their league. Adam just plays by his own rules. I opened my mouth to say as much, but then Izzi's lips twitched and her eyes roved all the way down to his toes and back up to his open, smiling face.

'You'll do,' she added, with a hint of a purr in her tone.

I wasn't sure I liked that reaction any better, to be frank, but it wasn't the time to get into that.

Of course Adam just grinned all the more, so I aimed a well-timed jab with one of what he likes to call my 'pointy little elbows'. He dodged it, and I gave him the *please behave yourself* stare he usually aims at me.

I didn't have time to play games. In just a few moments I'd be seeing Nicholas. In his house. In the house I *might* one day want to become my house. My heart began to do the mambo. And not in the slow, sexy way they did it in *Dirty Dancing*. There were odd rhythms and missed beats all over the place. I captured some air, swallowed it down, and smoothed my skirt with my hands.

We were greeted by a well-groomed, discreet-looking man who conversed with Izzi in hushed tones. He nodded upstairs and I looked up the wide marble staircase to where Nicholas must be. When I looked back again the man was gone, and Izzi was answering a call on her phone.

'You came,' I said out of the side of my mouth to Adam.

He nodded and gazed nonchalantly around the room. 'Looks like it.'

I resumed the *behave* frown. I hate it when Adam gets like this. He knows I'm buzzing with curiosity about something, yet he refuses to be anything more than vague. However, I wasn't about to give up.

'What made your mind up?'

He shrugged and looked up the marble staircase, which was lined with art I probably couldn't afford and definitely didn't understand. 'I decided I'd better check out this Nicholas chap in person.' He squinted at an abstract painting made up of squares in varying shades of beige. Without looking 'round he added, 'To see if he's good enough for you.'

My irritation melted like a chocolate bar left on a hot car dashboard. I was suddenly very glad Adam was here, and not just because it saved me from Izzi's displeasure if I hadn't come up with a willing victim. It was moments like these when

I realised what a treasure Adam was. I hadn't steered the conversation or fished for that compliment; he'd produced it all on his own. No string-pulling on my part whatsoever. And the warmth it gave me was twice as sweet as if I'd wrung it from one of my lovelorn swains. My heartbeat steadied into four-four time, and I was about to hug his arm when a horrible thought occurred to me.

'You *are* coming on the weekend too? You're not just here today to spy, are you?'

Adam reclaimed the *please behave* look and I instantly mumbled an apology. I should have known better. Adam is an in-it-for-the-long-haul kind of guy—probably why he puts up with me—and he wouldn't have turned up today if he wasn't going to go through with the whole thing. I was just nervous. What was taking all this time? Was Nicholas even at home?

The discreet man, who must have been a butler of some sort, reappeared and waited patiently while Izzi finished her call and slid her phone into her handbag. I'd half-heard the end of it and gathered she'd been chivvying her girlfriends along, telling them to prise their tiny backsides out of bed and get down here pronto.

'Your brother is ready for you in the drawing room,' Mr Discreet said in a silky voice, then disappeared again.

I was tempted to shudder. If I ever got to be a significant part of Nicholas's life, I wasn't sure how I'd cope with *him*. He seemed to vanish in and out of thin air, and, frankly, manners *that* good are just plain creepy.

Izzi started off up the marble staircase and nodded for us to follow. With each step my head grew lighter and lighter. By the time I reached the top I was verging on dizzy. It was all so elegant, so refined and understated. And in comparison I felt I had all the subtlety and grace of a kids' cartoon. I suddenly wished I'd tried harder to eradicate the Cockney edge in my accent. I'd given up too quickly, frustrated that when I tried to emulate Izzi's effortless drawl I always ended up sounding like a parody of Celia Johnson in *Brief Encounter*.

I decided then that being cool, aloof and businesslike—namely, keeping my mouth shut unless absolutely necessary—would probably be in my best interests. Men like a woman who's mysterious, don't they? And this approach would give me another fortnight to work on those vowels of mine before the murder-mystery weekend. I'd dazzle Nicholas with my witty banter then.

Izzi led us into a large drawing room with tall, almost floor-to-ceiling sash windows, and elegant yet somehow minimalist furnishings in neutral tones. I held my breath and hovered by the doorway, overcome by uncharacteristic shyness. Nicholas was there, gazing out of the window on the right and looking all lean, sexy and slightly irritated, in dark grey trousers and a shirt unbuttoned at the neck. Even in casual attire he oozed class.

I knew at that moment that if I had a future with Nicholas I would never again have to fear the spectre of the velour jogging bottoms. Not only would I not have to worry about being old and lonely and sad, but I'd become all I'd been training myself to be for all these years. I wouldn't be dressing up any more. I'd rightfully inhabit a world of glamour and elegance, sliding into it with the ease of Cinderella trying on that glass slipper. I'd finally be able to look myself in the mirror without having to blink a few times to erase my mother's eyes.

Nicholas turned to face his sister, the frown he was wearing only making him seem more broody and Mr Darcy-ish.

He spoke in a low voice, but unfortunately for him his gorgeous high ceilings carried his words over to where Adam and I were standing by the door. 'I thought you were joking when you said you were bringing "the gang" over for a fitting for this weekend of yours.' He hardly glanced in my direction long enough to register my presence, let alone see how cute I was looking in my pretend Lilli Ann suit with the flared jacket.

Izzi just kissed him on the cheek and waved his objections away with an airy hand. 'Well, we're here now. So you might as well get it over and done with. If you shoo us away, you grumpy old thing, we'll just have to come back another time.'

To his credit, I saw a flicker of indulgent amusement in his eyes as he nodded grudgingly at Izzi, then strode across the room to greet us. He held out his hand for mine.

'Nice to meet you again…'

That pause—the one meaning he couldn't quite

remember my name—almost finished me off. I felt like one of those buildings that you see getting demolished on the evening news. For a few slow-motion seconds it felt as if nothing was happening, and then everything inside me started to slide downwards. I grinned widely, hoping the shockwave wasn't showing on the surface.

'Coreen,' I said, doing a pretty good job of sounding nonchalant, actually. 'Coreen Fraser. We met at Izzi's birthday bash.'

A pinprick of recognition registered in his eyes, and it was just enough to delay the almost inevitable collapse of my crumbling spirits.

'Oh, yes,' he said slowly. 'You're the girl who sells Izzi all those second-hand dresses she raves about.'

'Vintage clothing, actually,' a gruff voice beside me said. 'Coreen is an innovative and successful businesswoman.'

Nicholas's eyebrows raised and he turned his attention to Adam.

Seriously, what is it about men? Sometimes you get two of them into a room together and they have to turn everything into a competition for who's got the most testosterone. Of course

Adam's surly interjection hadn't helped things.
I really was going to have to have a word with
him about this big brother protectiveness thing. It
was starting to make him behave most strangely
at times.

'Adam Conrad,' he said, thrusting his hand forward.

Nicholas looked across at me, and then back
to Adam. I knew that look. It was a jumping-to-
conclusions kind of look, and it seemed as if I
was going to have to intercept swiftly before he
got the wrong idea.

'My very good *friend*,' I added sweetly, before
Nicholas had a chance to put two and two together and come up with a million and six. He
didn't, however, look either pleased or relieved,
as many men did when they found out Adam
and I were nothing more than pals. His features
hardly moved as he shook Adam's hand. There
might have been a slight squaring of his shoulders, but who *wouldn't* when Adam was giving
off such confrontational vibes? I was feeling a
bit like standing taller on my heels and punching
Adam on the nose myself.

Adam released Nicholas's hand, a hint of a satisfied smirk sparkling in his eyes, and Nicholas flexed his fingers almost imperceptibly. If we weren't in such elegant company I would have delivered that punch. Or at the very least put one of my pointy elbows to good use. I'd only chosen Adam for this weekend because I'd thought he'd be a help, rather than a hindrance, but I was starting to see the problem with not enlisting one of my 'puppies' instead. Mongrels have a nasty habit of having a mind of their own.

How strange. I realised as I saw the two men standing next to each other that I'd thought Nicholas was much taller than Adam, but they were practically eye to eye, and instead of seeming younger and scruffier and more laid-back in comparison to Nicholas, Adam looked rough around the edges, yes, but in a masculine, slightly dangerous way. I suddenly understood why my single girlfriends—and some of the not-so-single ones—had begged me to set them up with him.

Although Adam and Nicholas had stopped squashing each other's hands in a show of masculine strength, there was still an atmosphere of tension in the room. Probably all those male pheromones floating in the air. Unfortunately,

I've always been a little susceptible to the stuff, and I felt my neck grow warm and the little hairs at the back of my neck tickle. I blinked to snap myself out of it. Now was not the time to get all hot and bothered over Nicholas. I wanted to be cool and poised and professional, remember?

But even with my eyelids shut I could feel myself reacting to his nearness. My skin got too warm as the heat at my neck began to spread. My jacket suddenly felt a little *too* fitted. I decided that keeping my eyes closed, even for a second or so, was just magnifying the sensations, so I snapped them open again. Only, as everything swam back into focus, I discovered that it wasn't Nicholas I was standing opposite but Adam.

How odd. Nicholas must have moved.

Izzi flitted round the three of us like a some-what demented butterfly. 'Oh, this is going to be *so* much fun,' she gushed, dragging us all into the centre of the room. 'You first, Nicky!' she said, and shoved me at him. Thankfully I kept my balance.

Nicholas looked at me now, waiting, so I delved into my alligator bag, half expecting it to bite back, and produced my tape measure—not so much with a flourish this time as with a fumble.

Nicholas was looking down at me, a faint look of concern in his eyes. His gaze drifted to the tape measure and stayed there. 'How are you going to…? I mean, where do you want to…?'

It was the first time I'd seen him anything but slightly bored-looking, and it was actually quite sweet. I got a little carried away with the idea he might be just as affected by the idea of me getting my hands on him as I was, and I totally blame the resulting adrenaline surge for what I said next.

I grinned back at him, forgetting the whole *aloof* plan entirely. 'Don't worry,' I said, my voice coming out even huskier than usual. 'No need to do a striptease. I'm very experienced in doing it both dressed and undressed.'

See? That came out totally wrong. And for some unfathomable reason every time I tell a joke or make a funny comment it always brings out the Londoner in me. In our supremely elegant surroundings my words clanged off the walls, sounding crass instead of playful. I blushed and busied myself getting my notepad and pen out of my bag.

Izzi just hooted with laughter, and said something about it being 'classic Coreen'. I didn't look at Adam. He ribs me mercilessly when I put my patent heels in my mouth, usually both at once, and I didn't want to set him off and give Izzi even more encouragement. I concentrated on being belatedly poised and professional instead.

Finally I managed to get something right. I took all of Nicholas's measurements swiftly and efficiently. Well, not *all*. I took his word for it on the inside leg. And my hands didn't shake even once. I was very proud of myself. In fact I couldn't have been more composed if I'd been measuring up Gladys and Glynnis, the two second-hand mannequins that live in Coreen's Closet.

I moved onto Adam next, since I was in a man-measuring frame of mind, and that was when the delayed reaction hit. My ears began to tingle and I kept dropping my tape measure and forgetting the numbers so I had to start all over again. Thankfully Nicholas was deep in conversation with Izzi by then, and didn't see a thing.

Hmm. I stared at my notepad and compared

figures. It seemed Adam's shoulders *were* as broad as Nicholas's. Broader, in fact. Just goes to show how appearances can be deceptive.

Once I'd got started with the measuring, I didn't stop. The rest of Izzi's friends arrived while I was doing her bust measurement and she dashed off to greet them, almost taking me with her, connected by the tape measure, but I managed to wiggle free in time. There were a couple of floppy-haired ex-public schoolboys called Julian and Marcus, Izzi's best friend Jos, and, to my horror, mouldy old duck-faced, stick-thin Louisa Fanshawe. Nicholas suddenly stopped looking as if he was a caged lion pacing backwards and forwards, smiled microscopically, and sent for coffee and croissants.

I noticed when they arrived that Louisa only nibbled hers.

I hate girls who nibble things. Don't trust them. In my book, if you want to have a cake or some chocolate you should just have it. None of this gnawing at it like a hamster, pretending it wasn't the sort of thing you'd wolf down in one go if you were on your own, and then leaving it half eaten because you're supposedly too full up. My reasons for not having a croissant were purely professional, of course. It had nothing whatsoever to do with not wanting to look piggy. I mean, I could hardly leave greasy, flaky marks on everybody's clothes as I measured, could I?

I could tell as I was doing the last of the measuring that Izzi was revving up to something. She kept giggling to herself and pressing her fingers over her mouth. She'd announced earlier that she'd tell us which parts she'd assigned us today, and I was dying to know who I'd be.

As I wound my tape measure I let myself dream about playing the part of the debutante. The whole murder-mystery thing was to be set around a family gathering on a country estate, as far as I could tell. I guessed that Nicholas would probably end up as the heir to the family fortune, and I was desperate to play his devoted fiancée. I even had a midnight-blue floaty chiffon dress picked out that would really set off my colouring.

Izzi made a big show of gathering us all on two vast sofas that faced each other near the fireplace, and produced a little notebook and silver pencil from her bag.

'Boys first!' she exclaimed, and fixed her eyes on Julian.

It turned out he was going to play the carousing younger brother. Marcus slapped him on the back and almost made Julian choke on his coffee. 'That means you're actually going to have to talk to a girl!' he bellowed. Poor old Julian just blushed and stammered something about talking to girls on a fairly regular basis, actually.

Marcus was going to be the layabout best friend of the son and heir, to which he merely said, 'Nothing new there, then!' and slapped Julian twice as hard on the shoulder. He'd better be careful. From the looks Julian was giving him there might be a *second* murder at Izzi's weekend. An unplanned one.

When Izzi said that Adam was going to play the cousin, who happened to be a vicar, I almost snorted my coffee out through my nose. Oh, I was going to have such fun with him! I wondered if he'd let me give him false teeth and a bald wig.

That meant, of course, that Nicholas was to be just who he should be—Prince Charming, for want of a better description—and I was more than willing to step into the shoes of his devoted princess. I sighed and reached for a *pain au choc-olat*, completely forgetting myself.

If I'd thought Izzi was excited at dishing out the 'boy' parts, as she called them, she notched it up a gear when it came to us girls.

'I'm going to be Lady Southerby,' she said, clapping her hands loudly and waiting for us to all hoot and exclaim. 'Isn't it going to be wild! I'm going to be a crusty old matriarch and you're all going to have to do as I say!'

'Not much change there, then,' Marcus said again, as he rammed half a croissant into his mouth and sprayed crumbs everywhere.

Izzi was far too pleased with herself even to give him one of her withering looks. And then she turned to me.

My heart began to pound. I clasped my hands together on my knees and looked at her with wide, unblinking eyes.

'You're going to *love* your part, Coreen,' she said. 'I guarantee it's absolutely *perfect* for you.'

CHAPTER FIVE

Perhaps, Perhaps, Perhaps...

**Coreen's Confessions
No.5—I've worn red lipstick every day of
my life since I turned seventeen.**

'I STILL can't believe Izzi did that to me!' The corners of my mouth tugged downwards and made my bottom lip protrude slightly. 'I thought we were friends!'

Adam glanced over at me, but kept his attention on the road. Just as well, really, since we were hurtling around the M25 in his Range Rover. 'It's been two weeks, Coreen. You need to let it go.'

Okay, I *may* have mentioned my displeasure regarding the matter to Adam a few times already.

'It is what it is,' he added, with an annoying air of superiority. 'Sometimes life doesn't hand us what we want, so we have to find a way to make what we *have got* work to our advantage.'

I folded my arms across my chest and stared at the number plate of the car in front. 'Thank you for that bit of priceless wisdom, Socrates.'

Out of the corner of my eye, I could see Adam had lifted one eyebrow. I decided his character for the murder-mystery weekend was going to his head. He was being annoyingly serene in the face of my abject distress.

'I don't need you to get all philosophical on me,' I said sulkily. 'I need you to be…to be my…' What was the word I was looking for? It wouldn't dislodge itself from my memory banks.

'Your back-up?' he suggested.

Exactly! I told him as much.

His mouth straightened out of its ever-present smile. 'Always,' he said quietly. 'You know that.'

I sighed loudly and let my folded arms drop into my lap. Yes, I did know that.

Adam indicated and swiftly changed lanes to overtake a van. I held my breath, wishing I was behind the wheel instead. Adam might be steady and reliable in most aspects of his life, but none of that seemed to rub off on his driving. If my car had had a bigger boot we wouldn't be having this problem, but unfortunately my treasured Beetle didn't have the space for all this lovingly pressed vintage clothing.

He saw me tense up and chuckled under his breath. 'Just because I'm here this weekend to be your "back-up", it doesn't mean I can't have a little fun along the way too.' And he pressed harder on the accelerator, reaching a speed my poor little Volkswagen could only dream about.

'Mongrel,' I muttered, as I dug my fingernails into the edge of my seat.

'Drama queen,' he shot back.

I didn't have much of a defence to that, so I slumped back into the comfortable leather seat and tried to smooth down the little catches I'd made with my nails only seconds earlier before Adam noticed them.

'When did you get rid of Dolly?'

Dolly had been Adam's old Land Rover. Older even than my little car. He'd had her ever since I could remember. But when he'd come to pick me up that afternoon he'd arrived in a gleaming new Range Rover, with a glossy black exterior and parchment-coloured leather seats. It was *almost* sexy—at least as sexy as a giant hulk of a machine like that can be.

'Oh, I haven't got rid of the old girl,' Adam said, smiling to himself. 'But I need something a little more…confidence-inspiring…when I go to meet clients. And a vehicle that doesn't backfire rust and can get from A to B without the help of a recovery truck tends to help with that.'

I trailed a finger along the immaculately stitched seam on my seat. Dolly Mark Two was certainly very impressive. And rather expensive, I'd have guessed. How on earth had Adam managed to afford her? I hoped he hadn't sold a kidney or something.

The clock on the dashboard said twenty to three. Only fifteen minutes more and we'd be at Inglewood Manor. Everyone else was due to arrive around four, to get ready, but Adam and I were getting there early so I could hang the outfits in each of the guest's rooms and check that every last cufflink and clutch bag was present and correct.

Ugh. Thinking about what everyone was wearing just made me remember the fashion monstrosities that I was going to have to wear over the coming weekend, and that brought me both down to earth and back to square one.

I closed my eyes, shook my head and let out a loud huff. 'I still can't believe that Izzi—'

'Get over it, already!' Adam half-yelled, half-chuckled, cutting me off. I clamped my mouth shut and resumed my pout.

I suppose Izzi hadn't sabotaged my plans on purpose. She was just dying to get out of her glamorous clothes and play against type. She must have thought I'd be game for a laugh, ready to do the same. I really shouldn't be cross with her, but I had to be cross with someone, and she was the only one in the firing line at present.

Adam performed another bit of outrageous overtaking and then looked over at me. I grimaced back.

'Okay...' he said in conciliatory kind of voice. 'Maybe you have got a *little* bit of a point.' I didn't like his tone, for all its sympathy and understanding. When Adam stopped bantering and talked to me that way it only meant one thing— trouble.

He let out a soft chuckle as he clocked a large blue road sign up ahead. 'What was Izzi thinking when she cast a girl who changes her mind every ten seconds as *Constance*?'

I was too depressed to box his ears or give a witty comeback. I just sat in silence as Adam turned off the motorway and headed in the direction of Inglewood Manor.

Yep. That was my role for the whole weekend: Constance Michaels. The dowdy, frumpy sister of Adam's country vicar. Not a hint of silk or chiffon in Constance's wardrobe—oh, no. That was all going to rotten old Louisa. I was stuck with tweed and dreary floral prints. Sensible shoes and good, clean living. It was going to be dire. The only consolation was that as the Reverend Harry Michaels's sister I'd be able to give Adam all the ear-flicks and Chinese burns I wanted, and he wouldn't be able to complain.

As we turned off the main road and through an imposing set of gates I sat up straighter in my seat. We were finally there. But, rather than the sweeping drive through open parkland that I'd imagined, the road to the manor was lined with fir trees. I could half imagine that they'd picked up their skirts only moments before and run to stand on the edges of the drive, eager to see the approaching guests. Through their dark branches I glimpsed clipped lawns, rose gardens and finally a vast redbrick house.

It wasn't until we were almost directly in front of Inglewood Manor that the drive widened and split to circle an oval-shaped lawn dotted with miniature firs in the most beautiful assortment of shapes and sizes.

I'd seen pictures of Inglewood Manor before, of course. Had known that it was grand and elegant. But now that I was actually there I realised that this vast multi-roomed house was also very pretty, even though it rose to three storeys. The windows were long and perfectly proportioned, and the unusual parapet of stepped battlements and cones, along with twisting redbrick chimneys, gave the house a fairytale air.

It struck me that Nicholas Chatterton-Jones was a man with a very attractive guarantee. Generations of tradition cemented his feet to the ground; he'd been bred to stay put, to build a family not to tear it apart. Chatterton-Jones men didn't do runners. Never would. So why did that realisation make me feel more nervous, instead of more convinced I'd pinned my hopes on the right man?

Adam brought the car to a halt, switched it off, and turned his body to face me. 'Raring to go… *Constance*?'

I jabbed him in the shoulder with a fingernail. 'Just you remember that Socrates met a very nasty end. Poison, if I remember rightly. And this *is* a murder-mystery weekend.'

The corners of Adam's eyes crinkled. 'I hear the deadly draught was self-inflicted in that particular case.'

I ignored him. 'Bring the clothes in, will you?' I said, waving towards the boot, and then I opened the door, exited the car with an elegant sweep of my legs and walked off to the huge wooden front door, channelling every bit of Marilyn I could.

'Starting to understand what drove the poor bloke to it,' Adam muttered as he pulled his key out of the ignition and jumped out of the car.

The rest of the afternoon went in a bit of a blur. Before I'd even unpacked all the clothes the hordes descended, and rather than being able to concentrate on making what I'd got to wear work to my advantage suddenly it was, 'Coreen, can you do this zip up?' or 'Coreen, how do I put spats on?' Or a million and five other stupid questions.

I hardly had time to notice the lovely wood-panelled landing between the various bedrooms, or lose myself in the ornate plaster ceilings, elegant furnishings and antiques.

Izzi had decreed that no one should see anyone else before the Great Unveiling Ceremony. Under no circumstances were we allowed to fraternise before six o'clock cocktails, when the murder-mystery rigmarole was going to commence. As a result, I was the only one allowed to see anyone in full costume before the allotted hour, and I was rushed off my feet running errands, pinning hair, finding lost gloves. Marcus even had the gall to pat me on the bottom and ask me whether I could fetch him a cup of tea. I gave him a look that left him in no doubt as to where I would *insert* that cup of tea if I ever returned with it.

I was most miffed with Izzi for laying down the law in this way. I had hoped I'd get at least half an hour to remind Nicholas just how gorgeous I was before Constance had to put in an appearance, but Izzi was into her character right from the get-go, cracking the whip and generally making sure we did nothing to spoil her elabo-rately planned fantasy weekend. I was starting to think the whole idea was more trouble than it was worth.

Finally, when I'd sorted out all the last-minute fashion glitches, I managed to scamper back to my room, close the door behind me and slump against it for a few seconds' rest. This was the sort of room you saw in posh interior decorating magazines, and I could hardly believe I'd get to sleep in it for two whole nights. Everything was elegant cream and muted duck-egg blue. There was even a magnificent mahogany four-poster bed, so at least I could imagine I was a princess between midnight and dawn, if nowhere else this weekend.

I took in a few deep breaths, drinking in the serenity of my surroundings. I needed it. There was only a quarter of an hour left for me to get myself ready, and it was going to take half of that time to de-Coreen myself.

Taking off the fifties garb was easy enough, although I had a moment of mourning when I slid my feet out of my heels and sank them into the thick carpet. I looked at myself in the mirror.

My suspicions had been right. My usual style of bra definitely had too much *va-va-voom* for a tweedy female missionary wannabe, and I had to replace it with something much plainer.

I left my make-up until last. I'd never gone anywhere in broad daylight without my liquid liner 'wings' and my Crimson Minx red lippy. Not even to the corner shop on a late-night chocolate run.

I stared at myself in the mirror for a few seconds. Really stared. This would be the last time I'd look like me until late Sunday afternoon. Constance was going to take over until then. I could already hear her tutting at the crimson lipstick, so I held up a tissue to wipe it away. The tissue hovered less than a millimetre from my lips and then my hand dropped to my side.

I couldn't do it. Couldn't wipe that last piece of myself away with just a few swipes of a tissue.

The eyes would have to go first instead. I wouldn't have to watch myself. The liner needed a thorough scrub with a lotion-splodged bit of cotton wool, and I had to close my eyes to make sure I'd got into every corner. Once that was done

I opened my eyes again and had another go at eradicating the Crimson Minx.

Another false start.

Another tissue dropped straight into the bin with not even smudge of red on it. I had a feeling I could have gone on like this all afternoon, but noises on the landing jolted me out of my repetitive loop. Voices. From what I could make out, the others were now all ready and impatient to show off their glad rags.

After taking a deep breath, I plucked another tissue from the box on the dressing table and did what I had to do without letting myself stop to think, scrubbing hard with the tissue until there was no Minx left, just smooth, soft pink skin.

I looked up. Met myself in the mirror. It wasn't a pretty sight. There was black grit in the corners of my eyes and a faint red tinge to the skin around my lips, making it seem as if the ghost of a clown hovered about me.

And *she* was there. Looking back at me. Pleading with me.

I turned away quickly, unpinned my hair and brushed it through, then put on the ghastly olive-green tweed suit I'd intended to force on Louisa and slipped my feet into a pair of sensible brown lace-ups. I then picked up my compact and got to work on my face, not making eye-contact with myself again until I was finished. Until I was Constance, with her severe bun and pinched expression, and the reflection in the mirror was safe again.

I walked away from the dressing table and surveyed the damage in the full-length mirror in the *en-suite* bathroom. I dared myself to take every detail in, to face what I had made myself. Well, if Nicholas wanted 'less' he was certainly going to get it from me this weekend. And, since Louisa Fanshawe definitely was the 'more', that should put me at an advantage, shouldn't it? As I kept staring in the mirror I realised it wasn't so bad. I might be prim and proper and prissy on the outside, but now I'd recovered myself I could see my *inner* minx was alive and well and blazing out through my eyes.

There was a knock at the door and I almost jumped out of my skin. 'Who is it?' I called back.

'Me,' came a lazy rumble I couldn't help but recognise. Adam's voice always makes me think of long Sunday lie-ins and rumpled sheets.

I took one last look at Constance in the mirror, thinking I'd show her a thing or two this weekend, and then went to open the door.

I hadn't seen Adam at all since I'd starting primping and preening the other guests. I'd offered to help him, but he'd said that I bossed him around enough when he was fully dressed and he didn't need me doing it while he was in his boxers too. Impossible man. I was sure I wasn't that bad really.

When the door swung wide I don't know why I was so shocked. It wasn't as if I'd expected to see Adam in his soft, worn denim jeans and his usual just-fallen-out-of-bed hairstyle, but even though I'd picked out his clothes myself—the dove-grey suit, the brogues and dog-collared shirt—I wasn't prepared for the transformation. Too busy thinking about my own, I suppose.

I stepped backwards, letting Adam pass me and walk into the room. I'd always thought that vicars were supposed to be safe, almost gender-neutral kinds of creatures, but even with a nice suit on and his wayward hair smoothed down there was still a hint of…wickedness about him.

Not helped by the mischievous smile he wore as he looked me up and down.

The warmth in his eyes deepened. 'You look gorgeous,' he said, doing a credible job of keeping a straight face.

I rolled my eyes. 'I look like an over-stuffed olive,' I replied, gesturing with my eyes towards the jacket buttons straining at my chest. When I'd chosen this outfit I'd imagined Louisa looking really frumpy, with the too-large jacket hanging off her bony shoulders. It didn't look quite the same on me. I'd been particularly pleased with the thick pair of round-rimmed—

Glasses!

I'd almost forgotten them.

'Just you wait until you see the finishing touch!' I marched across to the dressing table, picked up the tortoiseshell specs and slid them on carelessly. One hinge was a little loose, and they wobbled precariously on the bridge of my nose. I turned and gave Adam a defiant look, daring him to contradict me.

He just ambled towards me, stopping when he was only inches away. Slowly he pulled his hands from his pockets and straightened the specs with a tiny nudge of his fingers at either edge, all the while smiling into my eyes. He must have got them at just the right focal length, because suddenly everything that had been blurry and off-kilter snapped into focus and I noticed for the first time how the warm conker in the centre of his irises melted into dark chocolate at the edges. He dropped the softest kiss on the tip of my nose and stepped back.

'I've always had a thing for girls who wear glasses,' he said in his Sunday morning voice.

I wanted to grin back at him, to thank him for knowing the right thing to say to make me feel better about my horrible tweedy costume, but my lips were temporarily glued shut.

At first all I'd wanted was for him to join me in my tweed-related ranting, but he'd sidestepped my invitation and done the opposite, making me feel warm and confident. He'd given me what I needed before I'd even known it myself. Just like the takeaways he brought me. But even as warmth seeped through me, I shivered a little too. Adam's unusual gift for cheering me up was lovely, but it was out of my control. Something I'd never be able to coax or tame. Something he could deprive me of if he wanted to. And on that level I didn't like it much.

'Ready?' he asked, and offered me his arm in an exaggerated formal manner.

I stood tall in my sensible heels, lifted my chin and placed my arm in his. This was no time to get maudlin.

'Born that way,' I said as we stepped through the door and headed downstairs.

I had a light-headed feeling as I walked down the vast carved oak staircase with Adam. I was aware of my laced-up feet treading on each broad step, of my hand skimming the banister, but I felt oddly disconnected from those sensations, and the excited murmuring of the other guests drifted up from the hall below in a muffled fog.

At the half-landing there was a tug on my sleeve. Adam's fingers lightly gripped my upper arm and he steered me to look over the banister.

'Look,' he whispered, his breath warm in my ear. 'Look at what you've accomplished.'

I blinked and was instantly back in my own body, totally aware of the warm pressure of his fingers on my arms and suddenly his words made sense.

Down below the rest of Izzi's party had gathered, all dressed top-to-toe in the outfits I'd put together. Outfits I'd scoured the markets and auction houses of London for. Clothes and accessories that had kept me awake into the small hours of the morning as I matched and paired and mentally sorted them. And when I'd finally drifted off I'd had weird convoluted dreams about pearl buttons, Oxford trousers and hat pins.

'Oh...' I said.

Just for a moment I had the strangest feeling I'd been catapulted eighty years into the past and was spying, ghost-like, on a real nineteen-thirties house party. Were these really the same people I'd measured and had breakfast with only a fortnight before?

I spotted Izzi first, her grey crimped wig drawing my eyes instantly. She was holding an ebony cane, but every time she got excited she forgot to lean on it and started gesticulating wildly instead.

My gaze only lingered on her for a second, because I instantly searched the group for Nicholas. He stood out, taller than the other two men, looking all dark and handsome and dashing. I can't say he looked an awful lot different. But what was I expecting? One could hardly expect perfection to improve upon itself.

Julian and Marcus had scrubbed up well, looking very dapper in their single-breasted suits, sharply creased trousers and stiff white collars. I'd done a good job. Satisfied, I moved my attention to the females of the group.

Jos was bobbing around in her maid's uniform, and flirting with Nicholas in a manner that would certainly get her sacked if she really was the 'help'. I tried not to look at Louisa. The bias-cut dress in burgundy silk I'd picked out for this evening looked far too good on her slender figure, and the finger waves framing her face just served to emphasise her amazing cheekbones, which even I had to admit were her *least* duck-like feature.

Izzi spotted Adam and me as we reached the bottom of the staircase and let out a squeal. 'Oh, look at you!' And then she shoved her cane into Julian's unready hands and raced across the marble-tiled hall to inspect us more closely. A rather unbecoming smile for an elderly lady crept across her mouth as she looked Adam up and down. 'Well, *hello*, Vicar,' she purred. 'Remind me to come and confess all my sins to you later. I'm afraid there are rather a lot. You won't be too shocked, will you?'

Adam grinned back. 'I'll do my very best not to be, but it depends just how naughty you've been.'

The eyelash bat and pout that Izzi gave him pushed things a little too far for my liking. I thought we were supposed to be in character, but she looked ready to dribble down the black high-necked dress I'd found her. I coughed, partly to draw her attention away from Adam, but mostly to save the taffeta from drool marks.

Izzi dragged her eyes from the Reverend Michaels and started to walk around me, plucking at my tweed jacket and inspecting every little detail. 'The transformation's amazing!' she muttered. 'I would hardly have recognised you!' As she came round to the front again, she spotted my glasses and let out another squeal. 'Isn't it a hoot?' she said, grabbing my hand and dragging me towards the rest of the group.

'I'm practically an owl,' I replied, rather deadpan.

'I just *knew* you'd be a good sport about this,' she half-whispered, half-giggled into my ear.

I didn't do anything to disillusion her. I needed to keep on Izzi's good side this weekend, didn't I?

Now we were all gathered, Izzi introduced the murder-mystery weekend organisers she'd hired, who were playing the parts of Lord Edward Southerby, Izzi's character's husband, and the housekeeper. They gave us a brief introduction to the weekend, which I mostly ignored, and then handed us large white envelopes with our characters' names on them.

We were then led through into the drawing room. I could see why Izzi had decided to 'borrow' the family home for the event. It was perfect. The Chatterton-Joneses' drawing room was chockablock with antique furniture, and stern-faced portraits were everywhere on the moss-green walls. The room was so huge that there wasn't only one seating area but various groupings of sofas and chairs, the largest of which was in the centre of the room, close to the stone fireplace. They were upholstered in a deep plum jacquard, half hidden by a million tapestried cushions in all shapes and sizes. Anywhere else this decorating style would have seemed haphazard and messy, but in the drawing room of Inglewood Manor it just softened the effect of the vast fireplace and the grand plasterwork ceiling, making the space seem both elegant and comfortable at once.

I eyed my white envelope suspiciously. I had a horrible feeling that whatever instructions were inside were going to send my plans into reverse. I already didn't like what I'd heard about the reason for our characters to be gathering this weekend. We were supposed to be celebrating the engagement of Rupert and Frances—Nicholas and Louisa's characters.

'Robert will serve us cocktails while we take a little time to read our character packs,' Izzi announced, then dropped into one of the plum armchairs and got straight into being Lady Southerby by fixing us all with her beady eyes.

'What would you like, miss?' a silky voice asked from behind my right ear. I almost jumped straight out of my tweed suit. I turned to find Mr

Discreet from Nicholas's house standing there. I pressed a hand on top of my thumping heart and gave him a long hard look.

'I wish you wouldn't do that,' I said, frowning. 'I thought you worked in the London house, anyway.'

Mr Discreet—or Robert, as I know knew he was called—didn't let his weariness with the whole situation show anywhere but his eyebrows, which drooped a little at the outer edges. 'Sir thought I might enjoy a weekend in the country and a chance to…' He paused, as if he couldn't quite bring himself to utter the words. 'To *dress up* and have a bit of *fun.*'

The eyebrows said otherwise. I suddenly felt a pang of sympathy for the poor blighter. I glanced across the room to where Nicholas and Louisa were standing by the fireplace. He was pointing out family photographs of when he was younger and she was cooing over them.

'What have you got that's got a bit of a kick to it?' I asked grimly.

I could have been mistaken, but I thought I saw a hint of a twitch in Robert's left cheek. 'Perhaps madam would care for a Gin Sling?'

'That sounds lovely. A Gin Sling it is.'

Robert gave a nod of approval, but before he'd got two steps away Izzi, who was still holding court from her armchair, announced, 'Oh, no. That won't do at all, Robert! We can't have the vicar's sister tipsy on hard liquor.' An evil glint appeared in her eye. 'None of the demon drink for you, Constance, dear!' she added loudly. 'You'll just have to have something *virgin*!' And then she collapsed into a fit of giggles, as if it was the funniest thing anyone had ever said.

Of course everyone else had stopped their chatter when she'd raised her voice, and now they all chuckled along with her. Even Nicholas. I just pushed my horrible tortoiseshell glasses up my nose and pretended I didn't mind at all. The last thing I was going to do was let it show that her judgement of me had stung. Somehow, without my heels and my lipstick on, I couldn't bat the comment away as I could have done if I'd been 'me'.

I suppose I should have been grateful. I've been on the receiving end of plenty of chat-up lines involving filthy-named cocktails in my time. At least this was a joke in the other direction. But the joke was still on me, and I didn't want anyone to think that the idea of me being anything *but* a floozy was hysterically funny. Just because I normally look the way I look, it doesn't mean I'm…*easy.*

Adam suddenly appeared at my side and put his arm round my waist. 'Well, if we're drinking in character,' he said, looking in Izzi's direction, 'I think *you* should hand that champagne to me and replace it with a tomato juice cocktail.'

I had to give Izzi her due. Whether it was class or privilege or cold hard cash that kept her armour-plated self-confidence intact, it was doing a terrific job. There wasn't even the hint of a dent in it as she laughed back at Adam, downed her champagne, and then ordered the tomato juice from Robert, who was still standing beside me, waiting for my revised order.

'Whatever you bring me is fine,' I told him.

'How about a Maiden's Prayer?' he said smoothly.

Izzi grinned and clapped her hands. 'Oh, yes! That sounds much more suitable.'

I ignored her and nodded my appreciation to Robert.

'Thank you,' I whispered to Adam, and then deposited myself with as much grace and dignity as I could muster at the end of one of the sofas.

I looked across the room at Louisa, all slender elegance and perfection. Nobody would have made that crack about *her*. She had that other-worldly kind of beauty that made men think of medieval princesses and cherubic waifs. Whereas I was an easy target. Blessed with a figure that meant I was always labelled the same way—even in tweed, for goodness' sake!

For a long time I'd thought my sex appeal was the source of all my power, but just then, just for the tiniest moment, I started to wonder if it might be a curse, if I might always be the object of lust but never of devotion…

No. That was stupid. Of course I inspired devotion. I had my *puppies*, after all. And what could be more devoted than a gorgeous little puppy? And with that thought I squashed the nasty, wriggling feeling of insecurity away and sat up tall.

Stupid stuffed-olive suit. It was messing with my head.

So I imagined myself out of my suit and into Louisa's dark blood satin. I imagined my lipstick back on and four-inch heels on my feet, and instantly I began to feel better. Things improved even more when I tasted the Maiden's Prayer that Robert brought me. One sip and I knew the drink hadn't been named for its innocence. More likely because supplication would be the only way of saving oneself after two or three of these little babies.

My envelope was still unopened in my hand, so I decided to delve inside and see what the rest of the weekend might be about. When I leafed through the sheets of paper I had to stop myself from groaning. Izzi, in her mad-doggish fever about her project, had timetabled the weekend to within an inch of its life. How was I going to convince Nicholas how low-maintenance and laid-back I was if we didn't get any down time to mingle?

Along with a lengthy itinerary of activities—both indoor and outdoor—designed to promote clue-solving, was a full character profile of Constance, a brief summary of the other house party guests and some personal objectives for the first part of the evening. I had one thing I needed to keep secret and another thing I needed to find out: why Harry, my big brother, had become so overprotective of me in the last few weeks.

I let out a sharp little laugh at that bit. Talk about life imitating art...or was it the other way 'round?

Adam had just plonked himself down beside me, in the space I'd mentally reserved for Nicholas, and he leaned over to try and read my sheet over my shoulder. 'What's so funny?'

I quickly rolled my papers up so he couldn't see anything. 'No peeking!' I told him, looking over the top of my little round specs.

'With those glasses on you're actually quite cute when you're being bossy.' Adam didn't sound chastised at all. 'I might just let you order me around a bit more when we get home—if you promise to keep them.'

See? There was no winning with Adam. He was, and always will be, completely untrainable.

Since my character notes were still rolled up in my hand, I swatted him on the nose with them. 'You're not taking this seriously,' I said. My gesture had the desired effect and he backed away, rubbing the bridge of his nose. 'You can't talk like that to me. It didn't sound a bit like how a brother would talk to his sister.'

Adam came as close to frowning as I'd ever seen him. 'Suppose I don't want to be your brother?'

I sighed and fixed my eyes on Nicholas and Louisa over by the fireplace, toasting their pretend engagement with champagne cocktails. 'Tough. We've got to make what fate's given us work to our advantage...remember?'

Adam's gaze followed mine and then he sank heavily back into the sofa cushions. 'What idiot told you that?'

I grinned at him. Strangely enough, he didn't grin back instantly, as he normally did. But I'm pretty persistent. I just kept going until one corner of his mouth tilted a tiny fraction.

'So...brother of mine...I'm supposed to be finding out why you've gone all prison warder on me in recent weeks. Care to spill the beans?'

Adam shook his head and waved his own big white envelope at me. 'Can't tell you. It's supposed to be a secret.'

'Adam Conrad! You've never kept a secret from me in your life!'

'But I'm Harry, remember?' He rubbed his nose again and I started to regret whacking him there. An awkward Adam was twice as infuriating as the regular one. He planted his feet firmly on the Persian rug and stood up. 'And, actually, Adam does know how to keep a secret—even from you.'

I shook my head and let out a low, disbelieving chuckle. 'No, he doesn't!'

His expression clouded over. 'If you knew about it, it wouldn't be a secret any more, would it?'

Before I could quiz him further, to find out whether he was actually pulling my leg or—rather alarmingly—telling the truth, he glanced across the room to where Jos was standing with Robert. By the look of Robert's eyebrows he wasn't too enamoured with his partner in crime.

'Now, if you'll excuse me,' Adam said loftily, 'I have to go and weasel some family secrets out of Ruby Coggins the parlour maid.'

CHAPTER SIX

Wishin' and Hopin'

**Coreen's Confessions
No.6—You know some people say they
can't see the wood for the trees? Sometimes
I can't even find the flipping forest.**

I ENDED up being seated between Julian and
Marcus at dinner. Nicholas was far, far away at
the end of the ridiculously long table, deep in
conversation with an enraptured Louisa. After
the first two courses I still knew absolutely nothing about Julian, and was more familiar than I
could ever wish to be with Marcus's rugby inju-
ries. I didn't even have Adam to joke with, because he was being monopolised by Jos further
down the table.

I toyed with the last of my lamb. I wasn't actually hungry, but pushing it around my plate

helped distract me from a lengthy and rather too-graphic account of Marcus's latest shoulder surgery. When I did look up briefly I caught the eye of the party organiser who was playing Lord Southerby. He glanced at Marcus, then gave me a sympathetic smile.

Dinner was so dull I was about to jump up on the polished walnut table and do the Lambeth Walk, just to entertain myself. Thankfully, that rash plan was scuppered before I could make a fool of myself, because the lights suddenly went out and, with no big-city light pollution to provide a warm glow at the windows, the whole room was plunged into utter darkness.

One of the girls screamed. Someone—I could tell it was Izzi—chuckled with barely restrained glee, and the great rubgy-playing oaf next to me started making childish 'spooky' noises.

I ignored all of that, too busy working on rash plan number two. I was trying to calculate if, under the cover of darkness, I had enough time to sprint 'round to where Nicholas was sitting, plant a smacker on him, and then make it back to my place before the lights came back on again. Unfortunately, just as I scraped my chair back and hitched up my skirts, the inevitable happened, and we all sat there, blinking at each other and looking around.

And then we saw it. Him.

Lord Southerby, face down in his lamb cutlets, with a dagger sticking out of his back.

We all gasped together, as if we'd shared the same intake of breath. Well, everyone except Louisa, that is. Now I knew who the screamer of the bunch was. I turned to give her a scornful look and found her clutching on to Nicholas, so close she was almost sitting on his lap. Before I looked away in disgust, unable to watch my dream man being all gentlemanly and protective, stoking her back with the flat of his long-fingered hand, I saw a flicker of smug satisfaction pass across her features, just before she burrowed her face in his shoulder and he put his arm round her.

Thinking murderous thoughts, I focused once again on the supposedly deceased Lord Southerby. The drama of the occasion was ruined slightly by the fact that, from my ringside seat, I could tell he was still breathing. The intermittent puffs of air from his half-submerged right nostril were making ripples in the port gravy.

Izzi tried to get an appropriate wobble in her voice as she asked Robert to call the police, but it was obvious she was far from distraught at her fake husband's death. In fact, she seemed to be enjoying herself immensely.

The actress-slash-party organiser who was playing the housekeeper entered and suggested we contaminate the crime scene as little as possible, then asked if we would like to retire to the drawing room for after-dinner drinks. Once we were all assembled there we were each handed a second white envelope, containing further information and objectives.

I discovered I was supposed to learn if Rupert's fiancée was just a gold-digger, why Rupert had been out-of-sorts recently, whether Lord Southerby had left me anything in his will, and why Giles…

I looked up and spotted Nicholas standing in the large bay window that led onto the terrace, momentarily separated from Limpet Louisa while Julian quizzed her on whatever list had been in his envelope. I watched as Adam walked over to him and they began talking.

There was a large, brass-horned gramophone nearby and I drifted off into a little fantasy...

An old seventy-eight was playing on the gramophone, a sentimental thirties love song made only more romantic by the rhythmic crackle of needle on vinyl. The French doors at the centre of the bay window were open, giving a tantalising glimpse of a moonlit terrace. Nicholas would come over and ask me to dance, offering his hand, and I would graciously accept. How we'd actually end up on the shadowy terrace was a bit fuzzy, but eventually we would be dancing cheek to cheek in the moonlight. Barely moving. Definitely touching.

The little bubble of magic I'd created inside my head popped as Robert ushered a shabbily dressed man into the room. It was apparent after a few moments that he was another of the murder-mystery team, playing the role of a slightly clueless detective sergeant. I accepted Robert's offer of a glass of port while the man summed up the case so far and offered a few suggestions about possible motives. We were then left to chat amongst ourselves, supposedly to wheedle more clues out of our fellow suspects, while he investigated the scene of the murder. When he returned he brought with him the murder weapon—an ornate gold letter-opener, which was quickly identified by Lady Southerby as being from her husband's study.

Unlike a proper investigation, in which suspects would be interviewed privately, Detective Sergeant Moffat questioned us in front of the group, and soon a picture of the late Lord Southerby began to emerge.

He'd been a strict parent, fickle with his attention, favouring his elder son Rupert over Giles, the younger brother. He'd also been an inveterate womaniser and there were hints of dodgy financial dealings in the past. The detective made a one-sided phone call to an imaginary family lawyer and then revealed that Lord Southerby had visited the lawyer only a fortnight earlier to discuss changing his will.

We did a good job of keeping in character for a while, but once the sergeant had left and we were allowed to question each other the masks slipped and we started chatting informally, dropping our aliases and talking about last week's football results, next season's fashion and generally getting to know each other. All except Izzi, who remained stiff-backed and fierce-looking in her winged armchair, and refused to answer to anything but 'Lady Southerby' or 'Evangeline'.

I slid my horrendous glasses off and hid them behind a photograph of Nicholas as a serious-looking toddler on the mantelpiece. Then I subtly worked my way around the room, asking carefully worded questions of the different 'suspects' until I was close to the group in the bay window and waited for a gap in the conversation.

Remembering what Adam had said about *less is more*, I did a rather demure version of my eyelash sweep and tilted my head fetchingly to one side. Much less obvious, I thought.

'Cousin Rupert, let me offer my condolences on your loss.'

I placed my fingers lightly on his arm and left them there.

Nicholas turned and looked at me. I hoped he was just very good at acting, because his eyes were alarmingly blank. 'Thank you.'

I inhaled gently. Gently, because I was trying to make sure the top button on my jacket, which rested right at the fullest part of my bust, didn't pop off and give me a black eye.

'But I'm curious about something. Lord Southerby—I mean, Uncle Edward—always had a soft spot for me. You wouldn't happen to know why that was?'

Marcus let out a huge guffaw. 'It's obvious that the old rogue was a complete scoundrel with the ladies...' He looked me up and down, and suddenly my tweed suit felt as transparent as muslin. 'I can think of a *couple* of good reasons why,' he added, fixing his gaze on my straining button.

Nicholas, however, didn't even *try* to stare at my chest. 'I believe my father had some other reason for favouring you,' he said cryptically, 'but beyond that I'm not prepared to say.'

Adam looked at Nicholas, then across to me and back again. 'I don't suppose it had anything to do with the meeting your father had with his solicitor, did it? I don't like anyone suggesting my...*sister*...would do anything improper.'

Nicholas blinked slowly, and smiled a little, but it wasn't the kind of smile where the corners of the mouth turned up. His lips merely stretched wider and flattened. 'Possibly...' He looked down at me—at least it felt that way. I seemed a lot shorter to myself without my heels. At last I could see something other than complete uninterest in Nicholas's eyes. 'I'm sorry if I said anything untoward, cousin. I didn't mean to imply you were that kind of girl.'

I sucked a breath in through my nostrils and held it, only letting it out again as a wide smile blossomed on my face. I totally forget to do my normal Marlilyn-esque, parted lips thing, and just gave him the biggest, cheesiest grin in my repertoire. It's not often that people assume I'm not That Kind Of Girl, and I liked the idea that Nicholas was being careful of my honour.

He seemed taken aback by my wide-toothed display of gratitude for a second, but then he smiled back at me—properly smiled—and I saw a glimmer of *something* banish the greyness from his gaze.

'Bah. I've had enough of this foraging for clues nonsense,' Marcus bellowed suddenly. 'I think it's high time we all went off duty!'

Much to my displeasure, the rest of the guests seemed to agree, and our small group peeled apart and headed back to the sofas, where Robert was serving brandy. The rest of the group caught up with each other's news, chatting about friends I'd never heard of and relatives I'd rather not have heard of. After a long while the conversation dried up, and they remembered that Adam and I were sitting in the room and turned their attention to us.

Louisa fixed her gaze on Adam, who was lounging comfortably in the corner of one of the sofas, a goldfish bowl of a brandy glass held loosely in his fingers. 'What is it you do, Adam? And please don't tell me you work in an office like the rest of these poor chaps.'

Adam smiled at Louisa and shook his head. 'It didn't start out that way, but I'm finding myself office-bound more and more. I own my own company and we build outdoor structures.'

Before he could carry on I piped up on his behalf. I blame it on the fact I'd been left out of the conversation for so long, because the words left my mouth like a jack out of a box. 'It all started when he was fifteen and built himself a treehouse to hide away from his three sisters in the back garden.'

'Oh.' Louisa didn't seem quite as impressed by

the non-office job now. She smiled at Adam, but her eyes were flat and dull. 'How nice for you... to make a living out of something that used to be a hobby.'

'If only I could do that,' moaned Jos, who, despite still being in her maid's uniform, had flopped down in a comfy armchair and joined the rest of us. 'I've dreamed all my life that someone would pay me to lie in bed until noon and then shop all afternoon!'

I think the topic might have been dropped then if not for Julian. He lifted his gaze off his shoes and asked Adam, quite earnestly, 'And what kind of outdoor structures do you build now, Adam?'

All of them swivelled their heads to look at him, as if he'd broken some unspoken rule.

Julian flushed, but held his ground. 'Mother's been talking about replacing the old summerhouse.' He took a big swig of his sherry, then cemented his gaze back on his brogues.

Adam, however, wasn't gazing anywhere but straight back into the eyes of those judging him, not perturbed in the least about the lack of enthusiasm for his chosen profession.

'Actually,' he said, shooting a meaningful

glance at me, 'it would be more accurate to say that my company specialises in custom-built wooden structures—lodges, garden buildings. Our most popular range is luxury treehouses.'

'Treehouses?' Louisa's immaculately plucked eyebrows almost disappeared under her hairline. 'How quaint! For children, I presume...?'

All eyes now turned to Adam.

'Some,' he replied, with the trademark twinkle in his eye. 'But you wouldn't believe how many grown-ups harbour fantasies about having a treehouse all of their own, somewhere to escape when life gets too hectic.'

There was a general murmur of agreement and nodding of heads.

'But surely you don't mean *luxury* luxury?' Louisa said.

Honestly, I didn't know what her problem was. Couldn't she just let it drop and admit she'd been a wee bit patronising about Adam's 'hobby'?

Like you've been, a needly little voice in the back of my head whispered. *You don't really take much interest any more, do you? Too full of your own business, your own enterprises.*

I silenced the voice with a swig of vintage port.

Adam's twinkling eyes turned steely. 'That's what luxury usually means, doesn't it?'

Louisa gave a fake little laugh. 'But a treehouse is always going to be a bit...*basic*, isn't it?'

'Hang on a second...' Izzi said, forgetting to stay in character for the first time that evening. 'Do you mean the kind of thing Michael Dove has just had built? There was a feature on his new mansion in one of the Sunday magazines the other week.'

Jos leaned forward. 'Michael Dove? The rock star?' she asked in a breathy, hallowed kind of voice.

Adam nodded. 'That was one of mine. And it was great fun to build—two rooms, complete with bathroom, kitchenette, home cinema system and audio gear that will wake the neighbours three miles away. He said he wanted a guest house with a difference.'

'Up a tree?' Louisa said, still not quite getting it.

Adam helped her out. 'Up several trees, actually. We set it between three large pine trees at the bottom of his lawn.'

'Bloody hell,' Marcus rumbled. 'How much would a pad like that set you back?'

Izzi, with the extensive knowledge gleaned from the magazine article, mentioned a price that rivalled the cost of my one-bedroomed broom cupboard in Lewisham.

I took a sip of my port to steady myself, and ended up inhaling rather than swallowing. The choking fit that followed was in no way ladylike. Adam gently led me outside into the hall, so I could hack my guts up without an audience, and motioned for Robert to fetch me a glass of water quick-smart.

When I could finally breathe again, I straightened and looked at the man I'd thought I knew everything about. 'Why didn't you tell me business was going so well?' I croaked.

Adam gave me a look that was half-sad, half-affectionate. 'Coreen, I'm always telling you about my work.'

'But you've never boiled it down to a hard figure like that before. If you'd done that I would have paid a bit more attention!'

He pursed his lips slightly. 'You've never asked… Anyway, if you actually listened, instead of nodding and pretending you were, you'd have worked it out for yourself.'

My insides slumped like a fallen soufflé. With great effort I looked my Best Bud in the eye. 'I'm sorry,' I said. 'I should have listened. I should have known you'd take something ordinary like a garden shed and do something wonderful with it. And I should have paid attention—I'm supposed to be your friend.'

Robert chose that moment to return with my glass of water, and I took it from him, all the while looking at Adam, who was regarding me with a very un-Adam like expression.

Finally he bent down a little and kissed me softly on the forehead. 'It's time you ripped those polka-dot blinkers off. You'd be surprised what you'd see.'

And then he walked back into the drawing room, leaving me clutching the cold glass against my stomach.

I was right about there being a lake at the Chatterton-Joneses' estate. It lay beyond the formal gardens in artfully landscaped parkland. To the unobservant eye the small body of water might have seemed like a natural feature, but the diminutive island in the centre was almost painfully picturesque, and the weeping willows on the undulating banks were grouped together a little too harmoniously.

The blissful summer's afternoon only intensified the sense of perfection. The breeze was just right: cool enough to take the edge off the bright sun, but only just strong enough to whisper through the reeds and willows. Dragonflies flitted happily around us, tiny iridescent flashes above the water's surface.

I didn't care if all that beauty was man-made and planned. Primped and preened a little. Mother Nature is a woman too, and us girls know we need to emphasise our best assets. I didn't care if it was too perfect, either. *Perfect* was what I was here for, after all, and after the disastrous morning I'd had *perfect* was what I was determined to have.

After breakfast Izzi had frogmarched us through the woods on what was supposed to have been a restful country walk. There had been no mist—the clean sunshine had cut through the summer morning too well. There had been no bluebells—too late in the year, I discovered. No convenient rabbit hole. No being scooped into Nicholas's arms as if I weighed nothing more than a feather.

Instead Limpet Louisa had monopolised him the whole time.

I had to give her credit, though. She was good.

If I *could* have been objective, I might have applauded her strategy—one scheming woman saluting another. But I wasn't in the mood for being objective about that. Not in the slightest.

Izzi, meanwhile, had complained about all the 'out of character' chatter and behaviour the entire morning, and had moaned at us periodically for not having uncovered any significant clues yet. After lunch she'd announced her solution: a spot of boating, pairing us up with people we hadn't talked to much yet, so we could interrogate each other further. And that was how I came to be sitting in the stern of one of a row of beauti- fully varnished little rowing boats tied to a short wooden jetty.

As the boat bobbed up and down I could barely contain my excitement. Perfection was within my grasp. Izzi had finally done something right!

She'd paired me up with Nicholas, and in a few moments he would step into our little craft and row us off into Happily Ever After.

The setting couldn't have been more romantic if it had tried. There was warm sun, a cloudless forget-me-not sky, and all this achingly perfect scenery. There was even a pair of devoted swans orbiting each other at the edge of the dark green water. Surely this was a sign? Surely the scales would fall from Nicholas's eyes after this?

He walked along the jetty towards me, his long legs easily covering the distance in a matter of seconds, and then it was happening, just as I'd dreamed it would. Nicholas stepped into the boat and cast off, sat down, grasped the oars and rowed away from the jetty, leaving the others behind.

Nicholas and I were finally alone together.

I fixed my gaze on his strong arms and waited for that delicious tingle to skip from the base of my spine to the nape of my neck. Any moment now…

Okay, in a few seconds, maybe. Once we were away from the bank and he could build up speed, really pull on the oars…

I frowned and concentrated harder on his hands and wrists, since the rest of his arms were covered by his shirt and an off-white linen jacket, and I thought I felt a flicker of *something*. Unfortunately, after another few minutes, that flicker began to itch.

The *something* turned out to be a mosquito bite.

Flickers and tingles don't mean anything, I told myself. They weren't what I was there for. I was there to make Nicholas realise how irresistible I was, remember? The only one who should be *tingling* was Nicholas, and I needed to focus on that objective without getting distracted.

I decided my next step was to engage Nicholas in conversation, to show him I had brains as well as beauty. In fact, since the 'beauty' bit of me was still well hidden underneath Constance's tweed suit and specs, this was probably the perfect time.

We'd been told by the murder-mystery weekend organisers that we could reveal a piece of confidential information about our characters now, and I decided to set the ball rolling. I gave Nicholas a particularly enticing look and lowered my voice. 'I can tell you one of Constance's deep, dark secrets, if you like?'

For the first time since we'd left the jetty Nicholas took his focus off the oars and looked at me. 'Okay.'

I scanned the small lake, keeping an eye on the other couples in their boats. I suppose it might have looked as if I was being careful who overheard us, but actually I wanted to make sure the other couples were at a safe distance and that I still had Nicholas all to myself.

I looked into his deep blue eyes and my voice became even more husky. 'Well, this doesn't seem like anything much, but here goes… I have—or I should say, Constance has—a travel book about India hidden in her luggage. Apparently, she wants to go there to help the poor and needy, but her brother, Harry, has refused to help her raise cash for her passage or give a reference to the missionary society on her behalf, so she's planning it all in secret.'

Nicholas frowned. 'I presume she needs significant funds?'

I nodded. 'The missionary society will sort her out when she gets there, but she needs money for the boat—which I'm guessing must have been an arm and a leg in those days.'

He paused briefly, before taking another stroke with the oars. 'Could be a motive, I suppose...' He glanced over at Adam and Izzi's boat, which was gaining on us a little. Adam had taken his jacket off and rolled his shirtsleeves up to his elbows, and their little boat was zipping through the water. I could tell just by looking at Adam's back, just by the smooth grace of his oar-stroke, that he wasn't even rowing at full capacity.

Suddenly I felt all hot and unnecessary. I dabbed at my forehead with Constance's lace-edged hanky.

'Is the sun getting to you? You're quite fair-skinned, despite being a brunette,' Nicholas said, looking deliciously concerned. 'I can row into the shade near the bank, if you'd prefer?'

I smiled demurely back at him. 'That would be marvellous,' I replied. Not only would I avoid looking all pink and sweaty, but it would take us away from the other boats—especially Marcus and Louisa, who had also started to head our direction.

Nicholas and I chatted about the murder-mystery weekend as he guided the boat into the shadows cast by the willows. I liked listening to him. He had a very analytical way of thinking. Not like me at all. My brain seems to flit from one subject to the next with worrying frequency—although I suppose the compensation is that I have the odd flash of right-brained brilliance now and then.

Nicholas frowned. 'So, why won't Harry hear of you going to India? And what has all of that got to do with Lord Southerby's murder?' he asked as he lifted the oars out of the water and let us drift further into the shade.

'I don't know.'

I tried to *drape*, but it just wasn't working. No matter what position I got myself in, it just wasn't comfortable. I glanced across at Izzi and Adam's boat. They were closer now. It wouldn't be long before they swept past us, making a circuit of the lake.

'I tried to get it out of Adam—I mean, Harry— last night, but he was annoyingly evasive.'

Nicholas nodded. 'Yes, I couldn't get any of the information I wanted out of him either. Very cagey. If he's hiding something, it's big.'

My eyes grew large and round. 'You think it might be him?' I whispered.

Nicholas turned to look at Adam. 'Maybe. Who would suspect a vicar? But *why*? What possible motive could he have?'

I balanced my elbows on my knees and looked at Nicholas. I liked him even better when he stopped looking bored and was actually engaged in something. That carved-in-stone expression he always wore had cracked a little and it made him look more alive.

I tried really hard to think about Constance and Harry, and why my fake brother might have killed his rich uncle, but I kept being dragged back to the here and now by a rather annoying detail.

The conditions were perfect. Nicholas and I were alone together, and he was even leaning forward, looking right into my eyes. I'd dreamed about a moment like this ever since Adam and I had gone rowing in Greenwich Park, but now I was living the actual fantasy something was missing.

Still no tingle.

I trailed a hand in the water and gave Nicholas a sideways look. 'I don't suppose you could you roll your sleeves up, could you?'

He stopped mulling over suspects and motives and looked at me in clear astonishment. 'I beg your pardon?'

I closed my eyes and shook my head a little. Even I didn't know how I was going to explain my way out of *that* outburst. I did my best.

'You must be getting awfully hot in that suit,' I said, sitting up straight again and doing my best to look concerned.

A microscopic frown pulled his brows together and stayed there while he carefully removed his jacket, folded it, and placed it on the wooden seat behind him. Adam wouldn't have done that. Adam would have shrugged out of his jacket in a jiffy and thrown it into a crumpled ball, leaving it wherever it fell. For some reason the neatly folded pale linen bothered me.

I became aware of other voices around us and looked round to see all three of the other rowing boats in our vicinity. Typical. Just as Nicholas started to roll up his sleeves, as well. How was I supposed to get my tingle going now, with all these onlookers?

'Ahoy, there!' Marcus yelled as his boat lurched in our direction.

I couldn't see his face, as his back was to us, but Louisa was looking very beady-eyed indeed down at her end of the boat. It didn't take much guessing to work out whose idea it had been to take a gentle row under the willows.

'Watch out, Marcus!'

Adam, who was maybe twenty feet away in his boat, had stopped rowing and yelled out. It was too late, though. People like Marcus ought to have rear-view mirrors on their dinghies. He didn't bother looking over his shoulder to see who was in his way; he just kept on rowing until he hit something.

And that something happened to be us. Our boat rocked and I had to grab onto the sides to stop myself from going head first into the murky green water. 'Oi!' I shouted, and then instantly regretted my obviously low-class outburst. I clapped my hand over my mouth.

Marcus was conveniently deaf to any criticism, though. 'Listen here, Nick,' he said, grabbing the edge of our boat with his puffy fingers. 'My iffy shoulder is playing me up, and Louisa here is refusing to take the oars.'

I wasn't surprised. Marcus's rugby days were

obviously over. What might have once been lean, hard bulk was now looking a bit flabby and squidgy. He must have weighed a ton.

'We'll have to give up on this rowing nonsense,' he added, looking none too crestfallen.

Izzi and Adam's boat had drifted closer now, and she must have heard his dissent. 'Rubbish, Marcus. Surely you can keep going?'

Marcus shook his head, then rubbed his right shoulder and moved his elbow backwards and forwards, as if that was supposed to prove a point of some kind. 'We'll have to swap around.'

'But that means one of the girls will have to row, and that's not really on, is it?' Nicholas said.

We all sat and looked at each other, our three boats haphazardly parked about twenty feet from the shore.

'I don't know how,' Louisa said, and did a good job of hiding a smile.

Nicholas looked across at his sister. 'You do, Izz.'

Izzi let out a hard laugh. 'In this get up?' she said, indicating the stiff black dress. 'It'd rip in a second.'

She was right, as well. As Lady Southerby's

clothes were supposed to be old-fashioned even for the thirties, that particular piece had to be about ninety years old, made of crêpe de chine, and wouldn't take much stress on its seams.

'That's okay,' Adam piped up. 'Coreen's excellent at rowing. I've seen her myself. Strong as an ox.'

I very nearly stood up in the boat to call Adam out on that one! Apart from the fact he'd just compared me to a rather unattractive, hefty-looking farm animal in public, he knew I wanted to spend time with Nicholas. What on earth was he playing at?

I glared at him, but he just gave me that annoyingly serene smile he'd adopted in return.

Just then he was pretty lucky he was a couple of boat lengths away, because I would have wrung his neck if it hadn't meant immersing myself in a freezing cold lake.

Then I became aware that no one was talking, and five pairs of eyes were on me. Nicholas was regarding me carefully.

'You don't have to do this if you don't want to,' he said, just as carefully.

I knew he was waiting for me to make a decision; I just didn't know which way he wanted me to choose. I looked round at the other faces— Louisa's triumphant smile, Izzi's pleading eyes, Adam's warm, brown gaze.

I shrugged and looked over at Marcus and Louisa's boat. 'All right, then. I'll swap.' If I swapped with Marcus I might not be with Nicholas, but I could make sure Louisa and I rowed to the other side of the lake and kept right out of his way.

Marcus and Nicholas worked to bring the boats side-by-side, but before I could argue Louisa nimbly stepped across from one boat to the other. 'You're such a star,' she said thinly. 'I don't think any of us wanted to go back indoors just yet. It's such a beautiful day.' And then she bestowed a glowing smile on Nicholas, who, as luck would have it, didn't smile back—he was looking at me instead.

'Sure about this, Coreen?'

'Yes,' I said, spurred on by something I saw in his expression. I don't know how, but I knew that he was impressed with me.

He gave me a brief nod, his expression warming further. 'Hold the boat steady, then, Marcus.'

I stood up, for once stupidly glad about Constance's sensible lace-ups, and prepared to plant one foot and then the other in Marcus's boat. Slow and steady was the plan. When the first part was done, and I was straddling both boats as elegantly as I could, I took a few moments to steady myself, aware of the growing silence as they all watched me. Even Adam and Izzi, who had drifted closer, weren't moving.

However, just as I lifted the second foot, and was balancing one-legged in the other boat, Marcus decided to ease his shoulder with another set of arm rotations. He missed me, but hit one of the oars, the end of which made jarring contact with Nicholas's boat. It also acted as a lever, pushing the sterns of both boats away from each other in a swinging arc.

The jolt from the oar and the sideways motion of the boat meant only one thing—I went from having one foot planted securely in each boat to not having *any* feet planted anywhere at all.

CHAPTER SEVEN

Can't Take My Eyes Off You

**Coreen's Confessions
No.7—As much as I hate to admit it, there is a time for fantasy and there is a time for looking facts (especially the numbers on the bathroom scales) in the face.**

THE water that had seemed so perfect and tranquil? Well, it was cold and smelly and far from perfect. As the murky green water closed over my head I panicked. I'm not proud about that, but it was surprisingly cold, given the glorious summer we'd been having, and then something slimy touched my leg.

I hadn't had time to think about closing my mouth before I'd fallen in, and lake water filled my mouth and nose. It was the same three-shades-dirtier-than-olive colour as the suit I was wearing and, believe me, the water tasted as good as the suit looked.

I flailed around, desperately trying to find the surface, but my hands hit something hard and ridged. It took me a couple of seconds to realise I was *under* one of the boats. I opened my eyes to see two fuzzy, hulking shapes above me and no obvious gap between them.

That was when I *really* started to freak out.

I kicked with my legs, propelling myself forwards and upwards, desperate to get to the surface. My head hit the hull of one of the boats and I let out a silent underwater yelp.

Then something grabbed my torso, pulling me sideways. I kicked and fought, the breath burning in my lungs. At least I did until my palm hit something soft, something that definitely wasn't boat or muddy lake-bed.

I realised I wasn't alone.

In some weird, slow-motion part of my brain I thought, *How romantic! He's jumped in to save me.* But the slicing pain in my chest wiped those musings away, replacing them with more primal urges.

I clung to him, dragging myself against him

as he pushed upwards, wrapping my arms and legs around him just before our heads broke the surface. After the billowing underwater silence the shouts and squeals of the rest of the boating party seemed sharp and deafening. I buried my face in the crook of his neck to muffle them.

Slowly, rational thought returned. I coughed and hiccupped, thinking that if I'd known this was all I had to do to get up close and personal with this finely-toned physique, I'd have hurled myself in the lake the moment I got here on Friday afternoon.

I could feel the graze of rough wet cotton against my cheek, could feel shoulder and back muscles hardening underneath my arms as I held on tight. I felt totally vulnerable, yet totally safe. I knew he had me, and that whatever happened he would never let me go.

Was it wrong that it was now I got my tingle?

Despite the freezing water, a strange, buzzing sensation raced up my legs, surged through my body and lifted the roots of my hair. All I cared about was clinging on to him, the feel of him, the breadth of him, the dream of him…

'Is she okay?'

The voice drifted above me, merging with other phrases of concern in different tones and pitches.

I was okay. Shaken. Wet. A little humiliated, maybe. But okay. However, I didn't seem able to open my mouth and tell him that.

And then it hit me.

The voice. The one flowing in the air above our heads. That safe-and-dry-in-one-of-the-boats kind of voice. It was Nicholas's.

Recognition hit me like a punch in the head. I *knew* this warm, hard shoulder I was resting my head on. I'd relied on it for most of my life, in fact. But the knowledge that it wasn't Nicholas I was hanging on to didn't change anything. I just clung to him all the harder.

'Coreen?' Adam whispered in my ear. '*Are* you okay?'

It was only then I noticed the pounding of his ribcage as it was pressed against mine, the hitches of breath between his words. I could almost believe he'd been as terrified as I had been. I raised my head to look at him, hair plastered over my eyes so I could only half see him through the sodden strands.

There was something fierce, something basic

and protective, in those usually cheery brown eyes. I shivered a little. The water temperature, which I'd hardly noticed since he'd grabbed me underwater, suddenly seemed to drop. I still couldn't prise my jaw open. Our gazes hooked together and I nodded.

A flood of warmth replaced the fierceness in Adam's eyes. I loosened my grip on him a little, let my legs float downwards, but drew them up again quickly when they hit something soft and sludgy. It was then I realised I'd lost at least one of my shoes.

I also realised Adam wasn't kicking and splashing to keep us afloat, which meant that the sludgy stuff I'd felt with the tip of my toe… Yep. It was the lake-bed. My vocal cords ended their strike and I groaned aloud.

I'd thought I was drowning in just over five feet of water?

How humiliating! I couldn't even begin to look at the others, who were still peering over the edge of their rowing boats at us.

I sent Adam a begging look, no eyelash sweeps or tempting lip-bites included this time. I just telegraphed my desperation to him. Eye to eye. Friend to friend. Woman to man.

He didn't even blink. 'Let's get out of this over-sized paddling pool, shall we?' And then he hooked one arm under my knees and started wading towards dry ground.

Thankfully we were close to a section of bank that wasn't engulfed in reeds, even though it had flattened into a rather small and very muddy beach. Adam just walked right out of the water—although how he managed to do it with me, my curves, and my water-logged tweed suit I'll never know.

Once we were back on dry land I tried to slip out of his grasp and put my feet on the beach, but Adam stopped me with a firm squeeze and a stern look. 'You've got no shoes,' he said grimly. I hoped desperately that the strain I could both hear in his voice and see on his face didn't have anything to do with the effort of keeping me aloft.

'You can't carry me back to the house,' I squeaked. 'It'll kill you!'

Adam planted his feet firmly on the grass and twisted round to shout to the others, swinging me with him and yelling that he was taking me back to Inglewood Manor.

What a pair we must have looked, dripping wet, smeared with mud, and covered with tiny flecks of bright green duckweed. I hid my face in his damp, white and, now that I noticed it, slightly see-through shirt—which prompted a Mr Darcy flashback so intense that my legs began to shake. It was just as well Adam had decided against plonking me on the ground after all.

And then I was bumping gently against his chest as he strode across the grass towards the formal gardens that encircled the house.

'I can walk…really,' I said weakly.

'Shut up, Coreen.' He puffed the words out above my head.

I'd thought offering was the right thing to do, but was secretly glad Adam had refused. If I hadn't been feeling horrendously sorry for him, having to heft me all that way, I might have let the drama of the moment get to me. I don't get to play the damsel in distress very often—not for real, anyway—and I was tempted to enjoy it as long as it lasted.

I snuck a look over Adam's shoulder, wondering if the soggy, slightly smelly and muddy reality of what had just happened might look a little bit romantic to our audience, who were now some distance away. I also wondered if Nicholas might be even the tiniest bit jealous.

Wow.

That was odd.

For the first time in two months the thought of Nicholas Chatterton-Jones hadn't sucked a sigh from my lungs. It hadn't filled me with warmth because that glow had been snuffed out by a rather important question: why hadn't *he* been the one to jump in and save me? He'd been a heck of a lot closer than Adam.

The thrill wore off a little at that moment. Enough to make me feel sorry for myself, anyway.

'I'm so humiliated,' I mumbled against Adam's shoulder.

'If anyone should be humiliated it should be Louisa and Marcus.' Adam took a few more steps before he explained. 'She was sneaky and selfish, asking you to lug that big lump around the lake instead of letting Nicholas do it. And Marcus— well, he's just…'

'A plonker?' I suggested.

Laughter rumbled against Adam's ribcage, and

that delicious vibration made my chilly self warm a little. I hooked my hands more securely around his neck.

'Couldn't have said it better myself.' He smiled down at me. 'Anyway…look on the bright side.'

There was a bright side to being wet, smelly and utterly embarrassed?

'Well, first of all, the glasses have gone for good.'

My fingers flew up to my face and I realised he was right. My face was bare; I just hadn't noticed in all the kerfuffle.

'I'm a bit disappointed about that myself, actually,' he added. 'And, secondly, there's no way you can rescue this suit for the rest of the weekend. You're just going to have to find something else to wear.'

I lifted my head to look at him better. 'You're a genius! I knew there was a good reason I kept you around!'

I had a case full of 'spares' in my room. Vintage clothes could be very fragile, and I'd come prepared in case anyone spilled something down themselves or split a seam. Actually, there was a rather nice red dress I'd mentally ear-marked in case Louisa had such an emergency, but now I had an excuse to get out of the stuffed-olive suit I was claiming that dress as my own.

I rested my head against Adam again and sighed. We were at the edge of the rough grass now, just about to enter the rose garden near the back of the house. How had he got this far without dropping me? The tall, gangly teenager I'd known seemed to have hardened into a solid wall of muscle without me noticing. And that solid wall of muscle had gone awfully quiet.

'Adam?' I whispered.

There were a few seconds of silence before he answered, his words still slightly gruff, still laced with a smile. 'What now?'

I closed my eyes and inhaled the spicy after-shave that somehow hadn't been washed away by the dank lake water. 'I don't suppose I'm as light as a feather, am I?'

Well, a girl can dream, can't she?

He just laughed in the back of his throat, hitched me up a little higher and squeezed me closer to him. Me? I squeezed back, smiled to myself and enjoyed the ride.

* * *

I had the biggest, brightest smile on my face as I tripped down the large oak staircase an hour later. I was clean, smelling of some gorgeous shampoo and body lotion Izzi's parents kept in their guest rooms, and I was wearing the most divine red velvet dress. It wasn't halter-neck or backless, like Louisa's, but it was cute, with short flared sleeves, a long sash that tied under the bust, and its neckline was a wee bit daring.

Okay, Constance would probably have balked at the outfit—the V-neck plunged right into my considerable cleavage—but after the humiliation at the boating lake I deserved a confidence boost, and it was hardly as if I was dressed as an all-out vamp.

I looked up as I neared the bottom step and spotted Izzi there, scowling at me with hands on hips. I stopped bouncing from step to step and finished my journey a little more sedately.

'What in *heaven* are you wearing?' Izzi said.

I decided my best method of defence would be to bluff my way through this. I fiddled with the velvet sash. 'It's divine, isn't it?' Izzi opened her mouth, but I got in before her. 'Don't worry…it's authentic.'

Now I'd reached the floor of the entrance hall, Izzi grabbed me by the arm and propelled me through a dark panelled door into a small room—a study of some sort.

'I don't care about it being bloody authentic,' she said in a tight voice. 'It's not right for your character.'

I started to give a well-reasoned excuse for my attire, but stopped mid-flow when Izzi collapsed into an over-stuffed leather chair behind the antique desk.

'What does it matter, anyway?' she mumbled, sagging slightly. 'Nobody else is bothering to keep in character most of the time as it is. The whole blasted weekend is going to be a disaster, red dress or no red dress.'

I wanted to tell her it wasn't true, that we were all throwing ourselves into the murder-mystery weekend as hard as we could, but Izzi was right. I had only given thought to Constance, Harry and the grisly murder of Lord Southerby if it had helped me in my plans to snare her brother. I hadn't been thinking about Izzi and what she wanted from the weekend at all.

She waved a hand in the air. 'There are all these

stupid clues laid out around the house. Look, there's one—' She picked up an envelope addressed to Lord Southerby, which had been sitting rather obviously on a blotter in the centre of an otherwise empty desk. 'And do you think even one wretched clue has been found? No. Because everyone is too busy messing about.'

Her eyes started to glisten, and it made my stomach go cold. I'd never seen Izzi even *close* to tears before. I sat down on the edge of the desk and waited for her to look at me. 'But surely as well as solving the murder, the reason everyone is here is to enjoy themselves? Have some fun?'

The rest of Izzi's anger bled out of her face, leaving her looking closer to Lady Southerby's age than I'd have thought possible. 'Yes, I know. But how lame is it going to look when they all disappear back to London and tell their friends they went on murder-mystery weekend and nobody bothered to solve the murder?'

I swallowed. She had a point there.

'Take a good look at me, Coreen,' she said in a weary voice. 'I'm not like you.'

I was just about to tell her that was a good thing, but she cut me off with a roll of her eyes.

'I'm twenty-six and I have no qualifications to speak of. I can't run my own business, like you do. I couldn't even hold down a job! All I have is my reputation for being the most creative hostess in the South East of England. If this weekend is a disaster, I can kiss goodbye to all that.' She stopped fiddling with the clue envelope and placed it squarely back in the centre of the blotter on top of the desk. 'You're lucky you don't live in my world,' she said, sighing. 'The women are so vicious—always looking for an opportunity to trample you so they can be top dog—and in this world position is everything.'

She sat back in the desk chair and let out a dry laugh. 'I might be close to being useless, but at least I'm the *best* at it—you know what I mean?'

I smiled and nodded, and then I stood up.

Izzi looked worried. 'Where are you going?'

'I'm going back upstairs to change,' I said. 'And after that you and I are going to whip those layabouts into shape and make sure they not only catch the killer, but have the time of their lives doing it!'

* * *

Once again they were all staring at me, speech-less. It could have been the ugly beige floral dress I'd flung on, so I could run downstairs and catch them all before they went upstairs to get changed for dinner, but I suspected the silence was more a reaction to the lecture I'd just delivered on Getting the Most Out Of Your Murder-Mystery Weekend.

'Come on,' I said, in a slightly schoolmarmish voice. There were aspects of Constance's char-acter that lent themselves rather well to sever-ity, and I was quite enjoying myself. For once, a whole room full of people was taking me seri-ously. 'It'll be fun to dust a few of those mental cobwebs off and use our little grey cells for once. And don't these clothes just get you in the mood?'

There was a sheepish mumble from most of the group—all except Nicholas and Adam. The former was smiling and the latter was staring at me with an expression on his face that looked very much like pride.

Nicholas stood up. 'Well, if there are clues to be found round this draughty old house we'd better go and find them.'

Of course once Nicholas was on his feet everyone else followed. They put down their cocktails and headed for the hallway. As he passed by me Nicholas paused, placed his fingertips on my bare arm and bent forward to speak words intended for my ears only.

'Good on you,' he said. 'I thought this thing of Izzi's was going to be a total waste of time, but now I think I'm actually going to enjoy myself.'

I stood and watched him leave the room, my mouth hanging open slightly more than could be considered attractive.

Nicholas Chatterton-Jones had just touched me of his own free will. Miracles really did happen.

Izzi had decreed that this evening we would all wear formal dress to dinner—evening gowns for the girls and dinner suits for the boys. After an hour of clue-solving we'd all broken off to get ready, promising to get right back to sleuthing as soon as we could. As I came out of my room I spotted Adam, his hand on a doorknob on the first-floor landing.

'I don't think you're supposed to go in there,' I said, coming up behind him. 'I think that's Nicholas's room.'

He turned, his fingers stilled curled round the brass knob, and I had a reprise of the sensation I'd had when I'd first seen him in his costume yesterday evening, only this time it was ten times stronger. Adam and vintage dinner suits? They went together incredibly well. So well that my mouth dried.

'This isn't Lord Southerby's bedchamber?' he asked, frowning.

'No.' I shook my head gently. 'Next one along.'

There were only a certain number of rooms in Inglewood Manor earmarked for our weekend of sleuthing, and the weekend organisers had pre-pared and 'dressed' them carefully. The rest of the house was supposed to stay undisturbed. Just as well, really. Otherwise it would have taken us a month to search Inglewood Manor for clues.

A wicked grin lit up the face of the man who was *supposed* to be a vicar. 'Shall we take a peek anyway?'

I slapped his fingers away from the doorknob. And then I grabbed the hand that had touched him, clasped my other hand round it and hugged it to my chest. I'm not quite sure why I did that. I'd been slapping, elbowing, nudging and thumping Adam for most of my life and had never given it a second thought, but touching him just then had felt like crossing a line I hadn't realised had been there before.

'I was only kidding!' He rubbed his hand. 'And haven't you got all turbo-powered about mystery solving all of a sudden?'

'Turbo-powered is my middle name,' I said haughtily, and stalked along the landing to the right door. When I turned to look back at Adam, he hadn't moved.

'Don't I know it,' he said, a hint of hoarseness in his tone.

Now, I'm used to telling exactly *where* men's eyes have been resting while I've had my back to them. What's the point of perfecting a sway that reduces them to dribbling wrecks if you can't tell if it's had the desired effect?

Was it my imagination, or had Adam's eyes just flickered back from being much farther *south* than I'd expected them to be?

That awkward, not-sure-what-to-do-now feeling crashed back over me in a second wave, turning the thermostat in my cheeks to high. I waited for Adam to join me, and my hand felt slippery against the antique knob as I opened the heavy bedroom door and let it swing open.

I assumed he'd go past me, but he stopped opposite me, filling the rest of the doorframe. I don't think we were even remotely close to touching, but somehow it felt as if we were just about to. He stood there looking at me for a few seconds.

'I thought you were going to change.'

I looked down at the simple cream evening dress—not a patch on the red one hanging up in my room. It had short puff sleeves, a demure little collar, and beautiful little covered buttons than ran from waist to collarbone. I'd even been angelic enough to do all but the top four up, and my cleavage was completely going to waste.

It was obvious I *had* changed. But I hadn't ended up in the sort of dress I normally would have chosen, given half a chance. Was that what Adam meant?

'I did change,' I said, the tips of my arched eyebrows drawing together.

Adam didn't reply. He just looked at me. As if he was trying to see past the powder and foundation, past the restrained blusher and barely-there lipstick. As if he wanted to turn me inside out with the sheer weight of his stare. I slithered away from him, out of the doorway and into the room, and started hunting for clues, all the while feeling his eyes on me.

Eventually I turned and glared at him. 'Well, don't just stand there! Help me out!'

It didn't take us long to find an ancient-looking piece of paper, folded carefully and hidden in an otherwise empty bedside cabinet. I unfolded it and let my eyes rove over what looked like an old-fashioned birth certificate. Before I'd even read to the bottom, I gasped.

'It's mine! I mean Constance's! And look! There's a space where the father's name should be!' I turned to look at him. 'Does that mean what I think it means?'

Adam took the certificate from me and our fingers brushed.

It wasn't an accident. I'd done it on purpose.

And, from the way our gazes locked and held, so had he.

I held my breath while the air stilled around us and my heart bumped loudly in my ears. If this had been anyone else staring down at me, his eyes darkening, I would have sworn he was thinking about kissing me. Odder still, I wasn't the one to back away. It was Adam who wrenched his focus back onto the yellowing document.

'Of course we have to ask ourselves not just why there is a blank space where the father's name should be, but why a copy of your birth certificate is in Lord Southerby's bedroom in the first place,' he said, not looking at me.

I heard the words, but they slipped through my brain without taking root. Something weird was going on. It was as if I'd emerged from that lake into a parallel universe—a world that was deceptively similar, yet where 'normal' was a topsy-turvy version of itself. It made it very hard to think straight.

While I was trying to process the information Adam had given me, the dinner gong sounded somewhere in the distance. There were footsteps on the landing outside, and the sound of other people rushing back downstairs.

I waved the crinkly bit of paper in my hand. 'I finally have a clue,' I said, and folded it back into quarters once more. 'It's time we did something about it.'

Adam was giving me another one of his inside-out looks. And then he held out his hand. When I offered him the birth certificate he laughed, softly plucked it out of my fingers, and then slid it into his pocket. He repeated the gesture with his hand, and this time his large, warm fingers closed around mine.

'It's time,' he said, and kissed my knuckle ever so softly. Then he led me from the room. 'Time for us to see what new developments these revelations will bring.'

CHAPTER EIGHT

At Last

Coreen's Confessions
No.8—I don't sing very often, and certainly not in public.

ADAM and I were seated apart at dinner. Maybe that was just as well. I had said I was going to help Izzi make this weekend a success, and random thoughts about Adam—how he'd looked at me upstairs in the bedroom, how he'd held my hand all the way down the stairs—were interrupting my clue solving. It would have been even worse if we'd been sitting next to each other. It was as if there was a new Adam here, a different one from the boy I'd watched grow into a man. And, while I knew the old Adam pretty well, I had absolutely no idea what *this* one was going to do next.

By the time the main courses had been served

we'd hijacked the dinner table and made it our centre of investigations. It was amusing to see secret love letters, betting slips, a plastic revolver and a copy of Lord Southerby's last will and testament strewn amongst the bone china, crystal glasses and silver candlesticks.

I did a fairly good job of paying attention as questions and accusations were shot across the dinner table and deflected back with equal speed and vehemence, but every time I looked down the other end of the table I caught Adam looking at me. To the untrained observer he probably looked quite serious, but down in the depths of those warm brown eyes was a smile. A just-for-Coreen smile. And I didn't know what to do about it. Didn't know if I wanted to see it there or not. Didn't know if I was brave enough to ask myself what it meant.

I tried to ignore even the possibility of those questions by throwing myself into the investigation. We hadn't pieced it together yet, but one thing was certain—the late Lord Southerby had been a very, very naughty boy during his lifetime.

It seemed his sons had good reason to worry

about their inheritance, in danger as it was from money-grabbing illegitimate offspring and a gold-digging fiancée. Not only that, but Giles's rather unfortunate string of bad luck on the gee-gees had led to him dipping into the family fortune and then trying to cover his tracks.

Each and every one of us had a motive for wanting the lord of the manor dead, and those motives ranged from jealousy to greed, from revenge to the protection of loved ones. It was all quite thrilling, actually. We were still arguing about competing theories when we retired to the drawing room after desert. One camp thought Rupert had murdered his father, keen to inherit the lion's share of the family money before his father changed his will, and another group were sure it was poor little Ruby the parlour maid, who'd been fending off the old goat's unwanted advances for months now and had acted out of desperation to preserve her virtue and her income.

I looked across at Izzi, sitting once again in her high-backed winged armchair. She was smiling, watching a heated exchange between Marcus, of all people, and Jos, as they discussed the real reason for the discovery of Lord Southerby's bow tie in the maid's quarters. When Jos threatened to sue Marcus for defamation of character—and I think she half meant it—Izzi stepped in.

'How about some music, Jules? We could do with some light entertainment to help us let off steam.' She nodded towards the grand piano in the corner. 'I'm sure you know a tune or two from the right era.'

Julian actually smiled. He jumped up and headed over to the piano. 'I've rather been hoping you'd ask,' he said, pulling the stool out, flapping the tails of his jacket back and settling himself on it. 'I've practised a few specially.'

Izzi rapped with her cane on the floor. 'And there's no reason why you youngsters can't fox-trot later, or do whatever new-fangled dances you do nowadays. We can move the settees and clear a space near the bay window.' She fixed the rest of the men with her beady little eyes and rapped the cane once more. 'Well, hop to it, boys!'

Marcus paused, and I suspected he was going to pull the 'shoulder' excuse out of the bag again, but he took one look at Izzi and thought better of it.

Julian flexed his fingers and set to work, impressing us with a selection of tunes by the likes of Cole Porter and Irving Berlin. Mum had done a whole set of this type of songs once. Half of me didn't want to hear them. I hadn't been able to listen to her favourites for a long time after she'd died, and a familiar churning-in-the-pit-of-my-stomach feeling crept up on me.

But after the first pang of fear and grief I relaxed, welcomed those notes and melodies. Maybe it was because enough time had passed, or maybe it was because being Constance gave me some distance, but hearing the songs again now felt like meeting old friends. I could remember Mum singing them with appreciation and joy instead of fear and dread. Before long I was humming along and tapping on the arm of the sofa.

Marcus, who had been self-medicating his shoulder pain all evening with the contents of Inglewood Manor's wine cellar, drowned me out. I tried not to mind, but when he started to murder 'At Last', Mum's absolute favourite, getting all the lyrics wrong, I couldn't look at him. I turned away, still humming.

'You said your mother was a singer, didn't you?' Izzi said to me from her high-backed chair. 'Why don't you get up and sing it properly for us? It would save us from Marcus's warthog impression and I'd be forever grateful.'

Marcus had been lolling on one of the sofas while he'd been singing. He raised his head in inch. 'I'm doing a perfectly fine job, thank you very much.' He swigged back another mouthful of red wine and glared at me. 'But if madam here can do better, I'd like to see it.'

I shook my head. 'It wouldn't be becoming for a vicar's sister and would-be missionary to sing in public like that,' I said sweetly, hoping to put him off. Humming along was one thing; making a complete spectacle of myself was something else entirely.

He looked me up and down, his wandering gaze letting me know just how much *unlike* a vicar's sister he thought me. 'Pretend it's a hymn,' he said with a sneer.

I was tempted to get up and give him what for—that was what Coreen would have done— but Constance might have other ideas on the matter, and I didn't want to spoil Izzi's evening

when things had been going so well. As much as
it hurt, I was just about to meekly admit defeat
when a tug inside stopped me.

Constance Michaels might be a gauche twenty-
something who'd led a sheltered life, but she was
also prepared to trek halfway around the world
on her own to live in a strange land where she
didn't know anyone or even speak the language.
She wasn't afraid to look poverty and deprivation
in the eye and not turn away. She even had the
guts to do something about it. I reckon Constance
Michaels had a bit more gumption than I'd given
her credit for.

Besides, it was only Marcus, Julian, Izzi and I
who'd benefit from my performance. The other
four had wandered out onto the terrace with their
drinks after Robert had opened the French doors.

'You're on,' I said, then stood up and walked
over to the piano. Julian started the song again
and, before I even had a chance to get stage fright,
the introduction was over and I was singing.

I closed my eyes.

While I might not have had my mother's training, I had inherited her voice. I'd always shied
away from being like her, copying her in any

way, but now I was singing words that I had heard her sing so many times, and I felt as if it brought me closer to her. And not in a scary seeing-her-in-the-mirror kind of way. My mind was flooded with happy memories. Mum smiling and laughing and singing. And loving.

I remembered how happy she had been before my father had left, how her eyes had lit up and fixed on him when he was in the room. Even though it was only a memory I felt the warmth of her love. For the first time I understood her a little better, understood how intoxicating that feeling must have been, and how she'd have done just about anything to hang onto it.

My courage grew as I started the second verse and I opened my eyes. Bad idea. I'd discovered my audience had grown. Adam, Jos, Louisa and Nicholas were standing just inside the French doors, watching me with open curiosity. I thought I might choke, or trip over the words, but somehow I just kept on singing.

When I got to the bit about looking at someone for the first time and realising that you'd finally found that *someone*, that soul mate, I plucked up the courage to look over in their direction.

The expression in Nicholas's eyes was everything I had fantasised about seeing there, and I meant to hold his gaze and lock it down, but somehow I slid right past him and kept going, until I felt as if I'd run full pelt into a brick wall. Or was that just a pair of warm brown eyes?

My breathing went to pot and I missed a note. But then I had another one of those weird out-of-body experiences. Singing Coreen recovered nicely and kept going, her voice rich and smooth, but the other part of me was hardly aware of her, caught in a strange bubble where only two things weren't fuzzy and out of focus—

Adam.

And me.

I sang about smiling, and he smiled at me. I sang about magic, and he wove it around me just by holding my gaze. I sang about finding love, and something inside me warmed and melted. I couldn't tear my eyes away until the last note had been sung and the piano had fallen silent.

The song was over. The feeling had gone. I was back inside myself, standing with my back pressing against the piano, the applause of my fellow house guests ringing in my ears.

Izzi stood up from her armchair. 'I don't think we can top that,' she said. 'So why don't we stick some vinyl on the old gramophone and trip the light fantastic instead?' She nodded to Robert, who made it so.

Julian prised himself from the piano stool and, very bravely for him, kissed me on the cheek. When he stepped away I saw Nicholas walking towards me. He came right up to me and offered his hand. 'Would you do me the honour...?'

I nodded mutely and slid my hand into his. He led me to the space the men had cleared for dancing and drew me gently into his arms. Finally I was up-close-and-personal with Nicholas Chatterton-Jones. Exactly where I wanted to be.

I did.

Didn't I?

Everything about dancing with Nicholas was perfect. His hand was warm and sure on my back as he guided me round the impromptu dance floor. He talked easily to me, all the while looking effortlessly drool-worthy and smiling into my eyes.

It was perfect. It was.

Only...

I was reminded of those cakes in the coffee-shop display case that I always yearned for but which never seemed to fit the bill. Finally I'd found one that matched what my tastebuds craved. It had all the right ingredients, looked divine, but now I'd taken a bite I'd discovered that it tasted all...wrong.

Dancing with Nicholas wasn't a dream come true, it was an effort. What surprised me most was that I wasn't bitterly disappointed. Instead I had that horrible, warm scratchy feeling you get when you know there's somewhere else you need to be, something else you need to be doing. I was almost grateful to Louisa when the track on the gramophone changed and she nabbed the opportunity to cut in.

When I stepped out of Nicholas's hold I *knew* Adam was standing behind me, waiting for me to turn around and glide into his arms. And I couldn't stop myself.

'I didn't know you could sing like that,' he whispered into my ear, and a whole series of teeny-tiny fireworks detonated up the back of my neck.

I controlled the resulting quiver well enough

to answer him. 'You're not the only one to have secrets, Conrad.'

But I couldn't keep the banter up. The air around us seemed too heavy for our usual frivolity.

Adam didn't smile at me as we danced. He didn't even talk. If he had, I might not have heard him. All I was aware of was his strong, capable fingers holding mine, of his broad palm at the small of my back. I couldn't hold his gaze. It was too intense, too full of things I was scared to label, so when the needle on the gramophone scratched its way onto a slower song I rested my temple against his cheek and closed my eyes.

I have no idea how long we swayed and turned like that. Eventually, though, I noticed the air on my bare arms had become cooler, that the light behind my closed eyelids had dimmed to almost nothing. I flickered my lashes apart and opened my eyes.

We were on the terrace. In the moonlight. The warm yellow glow of the drawing room was only feet away, but it felt as if we were in a different world. The sheer curtains over the doors fluttered and curled in the light breeze, beckoning us back.

Silently, by mutual agreement and the meeting of eyes, we ignored their call.

Had we stopped dancing? I wasn't sure.

The way Adam looked at me…it brought tears to the backs of my eyes. Such gentleness. Such openness. Such *acceptance*. I couldn't breathe with the intensity of it. Something deep down inside me turned over. It felt like a door being opened.

Adam brought his hand up to the side of my face and his fingertips traced the line of my cheekbone, then threaded up past my temple into the soft waves of my hair. I knew what was coming, and yet I didn't know. Couldn't quite get myself to believe it was true, that it was Adam and me standing here in the moonlight like this. I stayed completely still.

He dipped his head forward and our lips touched, just for a moment, and then he pulled back slightly, so he was only millimetres away. I closed my eyes and let the weight of my head rest in his hand, and then I waited, a well of longing rising up within me. I didn't tease or taunt or dare. I surrendered. Maybe for the first time in my life.

And, as a reward, I got what I'd truly been longing for, because Adam really knew how to kiss. His lips brushed over mine slowly, teasing me, and then he deepened the kiss so swiftly I hardly knew what to do with myself. I felt as if I was falling and being caught all at the same time.

I lost myself. Along with all sense of time and gravity and reason.

And that's why I had to put an end to it.

That's why I had to push him away gently, my palms flattened on his chest.

Even so, it was *my* lips that clung as he drew away, *my* hands that bunched his shirt up into wrinkles before the cotton slipped through my fingers.

I blinked and looked at him. 'What was that for?'

Eyes of warm espresso with caramel running through them. I didn't have to look at his mouth to know he was smiling ever so faintly.

'You know why.'

My heart hiccupped. Did I? Did I know why? Certainly not in my conscious brain. That part was freaking out. But somewhere else, somewhere instinctual and primal, I knew that I knew.

I also knew I had to make sure those two parts of my brain never touched. Because if they did… well, I sensed there'd be trouble. And a whole heap of hurt.

Adam was watching me. I've been told that my emotions are easily readable in my face. From the way he was looking at me, I'd guess I was putting on a pretty good show.

'Okay,' he said quietly. 'Have it your way for now.' He didn't say more, but the words *later* and *soon* hung in the air around us.

My gaze floated off in the direction of the beckoning curtains. I could see Nicholas in the middle of the drawing room, no longer dancing with Louisa. He kept glancing into the darkness as he talked to Julian, but I had no idea if he could see us.

'You thought *he* was watching?'

The voice in my ear wasn't Adam's. Or at least it was a harder, steelier version of his. I snapped my head back round to face him. No caramel in those eyes now. Just gunsmoke.

'I…I…'

I didn't deny Adam's accusation. Partly because my tongue wasn't functioning well, still reeling

from the best kiss I'd had in years, and partly because on some gut level I knew it might be safer
to have an exit route. An exit route from what,
and to where, I wasn't sure, but the events of the
last ten minutes had been so bamboozling I was
operating purely on survival instinct.

He stepped towards me. Adam had never made
me feel even the slightest bit nervous before, but
this time I took half a step back even as my heart
began to thump in anticipation.

'I thought you were past playing games, Coreen,
but if that's the way you want it…' His eyes glittered and my heart-rate accelerated, race-car-
style. 'Let's make sure he gets a real eyeful.'

There was no tender touching of my face this
time, no gentle breath on my cheek. While the
last kiss had been soft and soul-churning this
one was angry and potent and—oh, my goodness—*hot*!

I didn't even have time to react as Adam yanked
me back into his arms. For a few seconds my
arms hung limp by my sides, my brain too overloaded with the information coming from my lips
to bother to send signals to something as mun-
dane as my arms and hands. But when the initial

onslaught of sensation was over I decided those hands and arms could come in pretty useful. I grabbed Adam either side of his neck, let one hand slide up into his hair, pressed myself against him and gave as good as I was getting.

He made a ragged groaning sound and it tipped me over the edge. I had no idea who was in control, and normally that would have bothered me, but if I'd been at a disadvantage at the beginning of this kiss, I now had a hunch we were both as lost as each other.

Eventually, though, the mist cleared. Right about the time I sensed a change in Adam. Right about the time he stiffened and wrenched himself out of my grasp.

I'd never seen him like this before. Where was my smiling, *twinkling*, comfortable and safe Adam? I didn't know if I wanted to swap him for one who could set my toes on fire with his kisses and yet look at me with such disgust. This one didn't seem safe at all.

He ran a hand through his slicked-down hair, returning it to its more familiar messiness, and shook his head. 'I'm such an idiot! Even after all these years...' He took a few steps backwards, his expression hardening further. 'That was quite a performance, Miss Fraser. You must really be desperate for this guy.' And then he pivoted round and strode away from me, along the terrace and round the corner of the house.

I ran after him. 'Adam? Adam!'

He stopped as I almost caught up with him and stood with his back to me, just breathing. No discreet floodlights here. Just Adam and me in the dark. I could only just see his outline against the blackness of the country night.

Slowly, he turned and faced me. 'What?' he asked, his voice low and weary.

My heart was thumping hard as I stepped to-wards him. I didn't have a plan, and I *always* had a plan when it came to men. It's impossible to train or manipulate or manage them without one. I was going on instinct again—something I wasn't entirely comfortable with when it came to the opposite sex—but my instincts seemed to be primed and ready, as I didn't even have to think before I lifted my hand to his face, mirroring his earlier gesture.

This was all new and I needed to explore him, to *discover* him.

I couldn't see his face, but I think he closed his eyes, and he made a noise as if he might be in pain. A few moments later his hand shot up and stilled my roving fingers.

'Coreen? Please...don't.'

I shushed him and turned his face fully towards mine, using my hand against his cheek as leverage. Then I pinned him up against the rough brick wall and kissed him back. There was no one else to impress. There never had been.

I lay in the dark in my peach silk pyjamas trimmed with lace. Yes, they weren't very Constance, but I'd reasoned if I couldn't be my glamorous self during the day I might as well make up for it in the privacy of my room at night.

I was alone, but I wasn't sure I wanted to be. Now, that was a scary thought.

Adam and me? Taking our relationship to that level? The thought made me shiver—in a good way *and* in a bad way.

He was my best friend. My Best Bud. *Could* that translate into something else? And what if it couldn't? Would we lose everything we'd built up over the years? If Adam's reaction when he thought I'd kissed him for Nicholas's benefit was anything to go by, I'd guess we just might. I wasn't sure I was prepared to take that risk.

But after this evening I also wasn't sure I could bear *not* to.

If I'd known Adam could kiss like that I might have done something about it years ago.

I rolled over and punched my pillow—more because my thoughts weren't letting me keep still rather than because the bed was uncomfortable. Far from it.

But you did know....

A memory hit me hard. Sharon Everidge's eighteenth birthday party. Her parents had hired a hall. I'd set my sights on Tom Morrison, the coolest boy in school, but he'd pretended not to notice me. I'd made him pay for that later, of course. But at the time I'd grabbed the one prop I had to hand—Adam. I'd kissed him. Kissed him the way I'd been wanting to kiss Tom, hoping it would show the other boy just what he was missing out on. But before long I'd forgotten all about Tom, and Sharon, and every other hormone-laced teenager at the party, because I'd been too busy kissing Adam.

It had worked. Tom had sidled up and asked me to dance with him not long after Adam had stormed out. I blushed with shame as I remembered that I'd gone, telling myself Adam would understand, that he was my friend and would want me to be happy. And, after all…it was only a kiss.

I'd been such a coward.

I *had* known.

I had known that Adam could make my ears tingle just by looking at me, that our friendship had the potential to blossom into much, much more. But I'd ignored that fact. Put my little polka-dot blinkers on and pretended nothing had changed, that nothing ever would or could change. And I'd been so convincing I'd even believed it myself. How stupid could a girl get?

That moment when I'd sashayed away with spotty old Tom Morrison had been a defining point in my relationship with Adam. I could see that now. Whatever might have been…or should have been…I'd put the brakes on it—too cowardly to admit what had been right under my nose all along.

In some subconscious area of my brain I'd

thought walking that path would be far too dangerous, so I'd clouded all of those warm feelings with friendship, insulated them, kept them safely at bay, and then I'd walked away from that idea. Heaven help me, I'd walked away.

And Adam had let me.

CHAPTER NINE

Body and Soul

**Coreen's Confessions
No.9—Nan says there's none so blind as
them that don't want to see. Why she keeps
harping on about it to me, I'll never know.**

QUESTIONS were still churning in my mind when
I woke, bleary-eyed and grumpy, the next morning. I reached over and bashed my travel alarm
clock so hard it bounced off the bedside table and
landed on the floor. The battery popped out of
the back and rolled under the bed.

Back then, had Adam realised what a mistake it
would be for us to get involved with each other?
Had he walked away from the idea too? And if
that had been his decision then would he make
the same one again today? Was history about to

repeat itself, with the shoe on the other foot? His foot instead of mine?

The breakfast gong sounded and I realised I didn't have time to stress about that now. I needed to get dressed, to make myself presentable. I launched myself out of bed and dived for the shapeless beige floral dress and baggy cardigan that were Constance's 'back-up' attire. I didn't even mourn the lack of four-inch heels, or—heaven help me—any kind of dart or tuck in the dress's bodice. I just forgot. And I didn't even remember to put on lipgloss before I headed downstairs to see what the fresh summer morning—and fate—had brought me.

I've never been good with delayed gratification, so breakfast almost killed me. I'd shot myself in the foot by delivering that lecture the evening before on embracing the fun of the weekend and staying in character. Adam was supposed to be my brother, and the minute I laid eyes on him I had decidedly unsisterly feelings for him.

From the look in his eyes I could see he was struggling too, but, Adam being Adam, he managed to talk and smile and eat his way through

it. Me? I just pouted and crossed my arms. When
Marcus leaned over and told me my attitude
that morning was somewhat unchristian, I was
tempted to ram a sausage up his nose.

Bizarrely enough, my glowing mood only
seemed to make Adam smile harder—the mongrel. I swear he was actually *enjoying* my dis-
comfort.

The next hour or so was torture. Izzi decreed
we were to scout Inglewood Manor for any remaining clues, as a few still hadn't been uncovered. In the process, we managed to rule poor
Ruby and the gold-digging fiancée out as suspects, but had added an over-protective mother
who might have killed her philandering husband
before he changed his will, leaving her two boys
with nothing, and a college graduate who was
in love with his best friend's fiancée and might
just have stabbed the wrong back when the lights
went out.

I hardly got to see Adam at all, with Izzi marching around giving us all orders and sending us
to different parts of the house. Whenever I was
within thirty feet of him he drew my gaze like a
magnet, and without fail he was already looking

204 SWEPT OFF HER STILETTOS

at me by the time I locked on to him. When we did get the chance to converse we had to do so as Constance and Harry, which meant keeping *on* topic, but hands *off* each other—which was all very trying.

'Come on!' shouted Izzi, rather like a general marshalling her troops. 'The will we found was a fake and the real one is hidden in the house somewhere. I suggest we look in the conservatory.'

Jos, who was standing beside me, sighed. 'Yes, because that's the obvious place to keep important paperwork,' she muttered, and trailed off after a striding Izzi.

I straightened my shoulders and followed her. After all, the quicker we solved this case, the quicker I'd have a chance to talk to Adam, or even have a few seconds to *think* about whether talking it over with Adam was a good idea.

The whole group trailed along behind its hostess as she led us through the entrance hall, through the library, and down a passageway past the kitchen that led to the football-field-sized conservatory. I would have followed her all the way, but a strong hand closed around my wrist, tugged me backwards, and suddenly everything went dark.

No, I hadn't fainted. Really, do I come across as the fainting kind?

There were a series of little storerooms along the passageway and I was inside one of them, a narrow shelf digging into my behind and my foot held captive by what I thought might be a string bag. No lights. Hardly any space. Pressed up against someone who was warm and breathing.

'Adam?' I whispered. 'Is that you?'

Dear Lord, I hoped it was Adam.

Mercifully, the pair of lips that found their way to my neck and worked their way upwards to my chin were heart-stoppingly familiar. I grabbed hold of his lapels, threw myself at him, and unleashed the whole force of the fantasies that had been running round my head since we'd parted the night before.

It was quite some time before I recovered enough to think as well as kiss. The first wave of desire retreated, readying itself for a second surge, and I took advantage of the moment of lucidity to pull apart from him, breathing unevenly, and rest my forehead on his shoulder.

I kept on whispering, even though the rest of our party was long gone. 'What are we doing, Adam?' I needed to know. Were we risking our friendship just to mess around and have a fling?

He laughed softly into my ear and I went hot and cold all over.

'I was under the impression you knew *exactly* what you were doing, but if you want me to walk you through it step by step...' He pressed his lips to the hollow between my collarbones and I gasped. 'I believe it started...like...this...' he muttered in between kisses, and I had to delve my hands into his hair, grab on and pull his head back to stop him. By the vibrations of his ribcage I could tell he was laughing silently, playing with me. I didn't know if I loved it or hated it.

'No, I mean...'

Another thing I discovered about Adam: he liked to play dirty. Obviously I hadn't been holding his head firmly enough, because he escaped and nipped gently at my left earlobe.

Oh, what the heck?

I let my head fall back, leaving him room to do

what he wanted, and indulged myself at the same time, skimming my hands across his back and shoulders, exploring the delicious dips where one muscle met the next with my fingertips. Adam's mouth found mine and I forgot to think about where my hands were or what my fingertips were up to.

'Constance? Harry?'

We both froze. That was Izzi's voice, and those were Izzi's hard-soled black boots on the flagstone passage. She walked right past us, calling our characters' names again, and then on towards the entrance hall.

I giggled against Adam's lips and felt him smile back. We'd been in this cupboard or pantry or whatever it was long enough now for my eyes to adjust to the darkness. A silver rectangle of light round the edges of the door gave just enough illumination for me to make out his features.

He pulled me to him, bunching my dress up near my hips as he made fists, and kissed me again. Slowly this time, with the earlier frantic pace giving way to something more languorous and sensual. I don't think I've ever been kissed with so much…feeling. It rocked me from the bottom of my stockinged feet to the tips of my unadorned eyelashes. I couldn't even speak when Adam had finished with me. One last, feather-soft teasing touch of his lips and then he rested his forehead against mine. I could feel his chest heaving beneath my fingers, hear him dragging in the still, dark air.

'You want to know what this is?' he said quietly. 'Where this is going?'

I nodded, keeping our foreheads in contact with each other.

'You were right,' he said, in his rumpled Sunday morning voice. 'I have a secret. One I've run from for years. And I've never told anyone. I've even hidden it from myself at times… But now it's time to open Pandora's Box and see what comes flying out.'

Oh, my. Adam wasn't secretly married, was he? Or suffering from a serious illness? I couldn't stand it if—

'Wh—what secret?' I stammered.

He kissed me again. I lost my balance and kicked a bag of what might have been potatoes.

'You.'

I wrinkled my brow. 'Huh?'

He stopped smiling then. I could feel it in the way his shoulders tensed, in the way his lips felt against my cheek as he whispered, '*You're* my secret, Coreen.'

My mouth opened but no words came out. To my utter horror, Adam's confession had filled me with more cold dread than if he'd said we were just fooling around, and I wasn't sure why. I didn't know what to say, how to respond, but luckily I didn't have to.

All of a sudden light pounded behind my eyes. I blinked and sheltered them with my hand. When I managed to make sense of what my forgotten retinas were telling me I saw Robert standing in the doorway, a jar of chutney in his hand, his mobile eyebrows hitched as high as I'd ever seen them at finding Adam and me wound around each other in what was clearly the pantry.

'Excuse me, miss,' Robert said in a level tone, and reached behind me to return the chutney to its home. He stepped back, but stopped with one hand on the door. 'I would close the door and tell myself I'd gone momentarily blind, miss, but I think I'd better warn you that Miss Isabella has been looking for you, and the likelihood of you remaining undiscovered is slim.'

I nodded and tried to straighten my wrinkled dress, still within the confines of Adam's arms. 'Thank you, Robert,' I said, in the most dignified voice I could muster.

'No problem, miss,' he said. 'I'll just push the door and give you a chance to…um…refresh your appearance.' He swung the door half closed, leaving a few inches of light for us, but I swear as he walked away I saw a naughty little smile on his face.

Another voice—a new one—echoed down the corridor. 'Talking to the jams and pickles again, Robert? I've told you before about the dangers of nipping at the cooking sherry.' The snorting laughter that followed identified its owner as Marcus.

Adam lifted his finger to his lips. I nodded and tried to silently smooth my hair back into a bun that was now only half there.

Sunshine filled the pantry once more. This time, however, Adam and I were ready. We were standing as far apart as we could in the confined space. My hands were clasped firmly in front of me, and Adam's were in his pockets. Didn't do us much good, though. I reckon Marcus rumbled us from the guilty expressions on our faces. Something had to have given us away.

If being caught alone together in a darkened panty wasn't enough, of course.

'Well, well, well…' Marcus said, taking every last detail in. I tried not to squirm, but to hold my head high and mimic that supercilious thing Robert did with his eyebrows. 'I thought you two were supposed to be brother and sister? How delightfully naughty.'

Adam grabbed my hand and pushed past Marcus into the passage. 'No,' he replied, giving the other man a stern look. 'Not brother and sister. Not in a million years.'

And then we escaped down the passageway into the unyielding brightness of the football pitch-slash-conservatory, where it seemed the sunny Sunday morning had been trapped and held to ransom.

The ancient woods on the fringes of the Chatterton-Joneses' estate were full of twisting oaks, fresh green glades, dappled sunshine and the kind of quiet that normally got on my nerves. The earth was springy underfoot, carpeted with a layer of old dried leaves and fallen pine cones. Adam and I walked slowly through it, side by side.

These were the same woods Izzi had marched us through only yesterday, but I'd been so focussed on Nicholas up ahead of me that I hadn't noticed how beautiful it all was, how perfect the stillness and quiet could be. I was starting to realise this wasn't the only thing I'd failed to see as I bulldozed my way through life.

Izzi's iron-clad timetable said we should all have some time to wander off on our own and meditate on the identity of Lord Southerby's killer before we met back in the drawing room for the big finale. Adam and I hadn't done much of that. We hadn't done much talking, full stop.

Breathless kissing? Hand-wandering? Yep. There'd been plenty of that going on.

It was so easy to be with him. To be like *this* with him. And that astounded me. I couldn't quite get my head around how our relationship seemed to have morphed seamlessly from one thing into another, and I had a horrible feeling it was all a shimmering mirage.

I couldn't take my eyes off Adam. While everything about him was comfortable and familiar, at the same time everything was new too. I'd never noticed the grace in his easy stride before, had never found myself staring at his sexy little dimples and marvelling at their perfection. That twinkle in his eye I'd always loved? Now I realised it was only for me. When it glittered at me I felt conspicuously giddy.

Why had I never seen any of this before? Why hadn't I *let* myself see any of this before? Each time this question wriggled through my thoughts and snuck its way to the front of the queue I sent it packing to the back of the line again. I didn't think I'd like any answer I could come up with.

I must have been frowning, because Adam stopped walking and turned to face me. 'What's up?' he said, his voice soft and low.

'I'm a little…freaked out by all of this.' I pressed my lips together and shook my head gently. 'I don't know. It's all so…'

His expression became serious and he reached for my hand and squeezed it. 'I *know* you, Coreen

Fraser.' The warmth in his eyes made my nose do that stinging thing again. 'I know just how much heartache you've had in your life—down to the very last ounce.'

I looked away, unable to look at the truth of what he'd said in his face. He waited while I sucked in air through my nostrils and attempted to quell the stinging. I didn't cry in front of people. Ever. Not the real kind of gluey, soggy tears that puffed my face up and ruined my eyeliner. I'm not proud to admit it, but I have squeezed a few perfect beads of moisture from the corner of my eye when the occasion demanded it, when it would help me get my own way. But I measured out my tears. I decided how many fell and when. I stayed in control always.

He carried on talking as I fixed my gaze on a holly bush and didn't turn back. 'I understand why relationships are something you've either deliberately avoided or sabotaged when they threatened to get too serious.'

Did he? I wished he'd tell *me*.

And I wished Adam couldn't see past the polka dots and lipstick. I wished he couldn't look inside me as if I was made of glass and tell me what the writing on my heart was when I couldn't even decipher it myself. I couldn't be mysterious and unpredictable with Adam. Those two things were my best weapons for keeping a man on his toes, for keeping him off balance while my stiletto heels were firmly anchored to the floor. And there wasn't even a fair trade-off with Adam. He knew everything about me, and I had missed even the most obvious things about him.

I turned my head back, but focused on one of the buttons on his shirt instead of looking him in the face. 'Do you think we're doing the right thing?' I asked. 'Whatever is going on between us could spell the end of our friendship.'

He held my chin softly between thumb and forefinger and tipped my face up. 'We've run from this for long enough, Coreen. I've loved being your friend, but I've finally admitted to myself that I want more, and I can't keep pretending that I don't. Don't ask me to go back.'

The force of his honesty sent me searching for that nice, safe button to fix my gaze on again. My instinct was to gloss over this difficult topic by doing any one of the hundred things I usually did in similar situations—like blowing a kiss and sashaying mysteriously away without answering—but I found myself disarmed. In the literal sense. The only thing I had left in my arsenal was candour.

I took a deep breath. 'I don't know if I'm ready for this.'

He stepped forward and closed his arms around me. Even in his dull grey vicar's suit he smelled amazing. I pressed my cheek against him. The shirt button was so close now I went cross-eyed trying to keep it sharp and in focus.

'You won't know unless you try, and I think you're ready for more than you give yourself credit for.'

My eyes started to ache and the button became blurry.

'How do you know? And how come you know when I don't know it myself?' I knew I sounded a bit sulky, but I couldn't help myself.

He leaned forward and kissed me. His lips were warm and soft and teasing. I made a noise that was suspiciously like a purr.

'Not fair,' I said, but I smiled at the same time.

I arched the top of my back so I could look at him. He wasn't smiling, but looking grave.

'When you started mooning over old Nicholas, I
knew it wasn't just another fleeting crush. I knew
this time it was different for you.'

I raised an eyebrow. 'Oh? Did you?'

'Yes, I did. And I decided it was time to explore
whatever has been simmering under the surface
between us for years. That thing we've always
pretended wasn't there. I realised I didn't want
you to want Nicholas. I wanted you to want *me*.'
One corner of his mouth twisted a little. 'That's
why I agreed to come on this weekend with you.
I had to do something to make that happen.'

I gave him a disbelieving look. 'So you're telling me *you* had a plan while I had none?'

'Sort of.' And then he grinned at me. That
caught-you-out-this-time grin I knew so well.

Even though my upper arms were pinned under
his more muscular ones, I wiggled a hand free
and thumped him on the chest. 'Insufferable big-
head!'

'Minx!' he whispered, then shut me up with
another heart-stopping kiss. When he drew away
he was chuckling under his breath. 'I think the
plan worked out rather well, don't you?'

I laughed too at first, but then I started to feel

uncomfortable. As much as I was beginning to enjoy the added sizzle to our old banter, I didn't like the idea of being a pawn moved around in someone else's game. I pushed my way out his arms and walked away.

'Don't play games with me,' I said over my shoulder.

Adam fell into step beside me, but I kept looking straight ahead. 'I'm not playing games with you. What I feel for you is real—and I don't think you're in any position to lecture me on game-playing, anyway.'

I spun around to face him. 'That was different! I didn't… They never meant…' I couldn't finish that sentence. Couldn't tell him this was on a completely different level to my little bag of tricks. What I did was harmless fun. The games Adam was playing could really get someone hurt.

'This isn't going to work! We're already fighting.'

He gave me a sharp look. 'Don't do this, Coreen. It *can* work…'

I shook my head and started backing away. 'This is all too much. Twenty-four hours ago we were just good friends—best friends!—and now you're asking me to decide my whole future. You're asking too much!'

Adam shook his head. 'I'm not asking for eternity! Just a chance.'

I could feel the tears collecting behind my eyes and I squashed my face up to deny them exit. 'It's already poisoning our friendship! And I *need* that from you. You're the one person in my life I can—'.

Trust.

Go on, Coreen. Say the word. It's only a tiny one. It can't be that hard.

I gulped. The tears were trying to find an alternative escape route—up my throat and down the back of my nose. I shook my head again, more vigorously this time.

'I'm not sure this is what I want,' was all I managed to mumble.

He tried to reach for me, but I stumbled further backwards, watching his jaw harden as I did so.

'And I can't keep pretending friendship is enough for me any more. I've lied to myself, and to you, for too long.' His stare was fierce, then he puffed out a breath and ran a hand through his hair before looking at me again.

'Maybe this has been too hot and fast and heavy. Maybe we do need to slow down.' He shoved his hands in his pockets. 'You want space? You've got it.' As he spoke his voice softened and the irritation melted away. That was harder to deal with, to be honest. He looked into my eyes. 'You know where I stand. Take some time to think about this—not just react to it—and when you know what you want, come and find me.'

He turned and walked off, his shoulders bunched, head low.

Me? I did what any self-respecting drama queen would do in my shoes. I ran in the opposite direction and didn't stop until I was out in the sunshine again and the unhealthy silence of the woods was far behind me.

We gathered at three in the drawing room. I didn't sit with Adam.

He didn't sulk, as I would have done. He talked with the other murder-mystery guests, and engaged in the proceedings, but every now and then he'd look at me and I'd feel heavy inside. There was no condemnation or accusation in his eyes, no sense of pressure. It only made me feel worse, because I really felt like throwing a wobbly to shake the awful lethargy that had settled on me, and I had nothing whatsoever to use as a justifiable trigger.

The shabby detective was back, and he laid the case out for us, summarising his interviews and our own interrogations of each other. Each clue had been clearly tagged and laid on the long cherrywood coffee table in the centre of the room.

I listened with one ear, but inside my head I was involved in a similar process. Sorting. Labelling. Remembering. My memory seemed determined to dredge up all sorts of strange little details. I didn't even recall storing them away, but there they were, all neatly labelled and catalogued, just like the detective's evidence…

The way Adam had always watched out for me and stood up for me, even when I'd still been in primary school. The way he was faithful and loyal now we were all grown up, despite my shenanigans. That playful glint in his eye when we argued, as if he enjoyed even that just because it was me he was sparring with. The way that playfulness had hardened into danger last night on the terrace.

After the general memories came the specifics. Thick and fast.

The bleakness in his eyes as he'd stood on his doorstep and listened to my apology after that fateful party. The squaring of his shoulders the first time he'd met Nicholas. The way he always inhaled deeply when he hugged me, as if he couldn't help himself breathing in my scent.

They were fragments, really. Nothing more than that. But when I pieced them together there was only one conclusion I could come to.

Adam loved me. Had done so for a long time. And I'm not sure either of us had really known.

I sat there on the sofa, staring at the plastic gun on the coffee table and trying to work out what that meant, how I felt about it. But I was numb. Overloaded. Terrified.

The others were asking questions of each other, bandying theories around and knocking each other's clever arguments to the floor with new insights, but I didn't hear any of it. My memory had cranked into gear again, and this time the images being flung in my direction, the sounds and words, all related to me.

My face lighting up every time I saw him, no

matter how glum I'd been before he walked in
the door. The way he made me feel as if I could
do anything, be anything. His hand my only
anchor at my mum's funeral, as we'd watched
four strangers in black carry her into the chapel.
I'd squeezed it so hard it had creaked for days
afterwards.

I'd needed him then, more than I could ex-
press or even comprehend. But I'd never had to
articulate those feelings. In fact I'd never had to
ask him for anything that I'd really *needed*. Oh,
I might have begged and wheedled and sulked to
get him to agree to something I *wanted*, but that
wasn't the same thing. He'd always been there,
ready with what I needed—like the takeaways.
I'd just been too blind to see that what I really
wanted, what I really needed, was him.

My gaze flew to his face. He was laughing with
Izzi about some ridiculous theory she'd just put
forward, his grin wide and his dimples creasing
deep in his cheeks, and suddenly I felt as if I were
falling. Not a gentle floating, but being dragged
by gravity so fast it sucked the breath from my
lungs, the words from my mouth. I felt clammy
and twitchy, shivery and cold.

And then I hit the bottom of whatever I'd been falling down. But instead of it ending with a nasty, messy *splat* there was an explosion of warmth and light. It rushed outwards from my ribcage until pins and needles stabbed my fingers and toes, until the roots of my hair tingled to attention.

Finally the polka-dots fell from my eyes.

I stood up shakily, my mouth working, my eyes wide. A couple of people stopped talking and stared at me.

'It's you,' I said to Adam across the room. 'It was you all along.'

He broke off mid-sentence and our gazes snagged and held.

There was a reedy voice to my left. The detective. 'Are you making a formal accusation?' he asked.

I nodded dumbly. How could I deny it?

He was the one. The cupcake of my dreams.

I was in love with my best friend.

I was in love with Adam Conrad.

CHAPTER TEN

Fever

**Coreen's Confessions
No.10—You might not believe it, but sometimes I take things too far.**

THE next twenty minutes were mayhem. Everyone talked over each other, unravelling the remaining tangles in the mystery we'd all been trying to solve. More than once I was clapped on the back and congratulated for working it out, but I hardly registered it.

I'd finally worked it out. But I wasn't clever. I was very, very stupid. The clues had been laid out for me, and all I'd had to do was take the focus off myself long enough to see them winking at me along the way. I never had. What did that say about me as a person?

I could see with such clarity now why I'd been

so territorial about Adam with my friends, why I
put up with his endless teasing. Why he felt like
a part of me. And it had only taken me the best
part of twenty years to work it all out.

Very, very stupid.

Stupid not to have seen it. Stupid to have allowed it to happen in the first place. By not opening my eyes to it, thinking that was the safer
option, I'd actually left myself even more vulnerable.

Jos and Louisa were making a fuss of Adam,
asking him how he'd managed to fool them all
weekend. Even Nicholas gave him a handshake.
Then they wanted to know what his motive
had been. It turned out my supposed brother—
brother? Hah!—had discovered his beloved
younger sister was the product of his uncle's
affair with their mother. The late Lord Southerby
had been getting sentimental in recent months,
had regretted denying paternity and had talked
about changing his will. Harry had been scared
for Constance, had sought to protect a young
woman who selflessly wanted to spend her life
helping others from a scandal that would pre-
vent her from doing just that. What missionary

society would have sent the illegitimate daughter of a well-known cad overseas as an example of good Christian morals? Harry had acted out of love and rage and retribution.

I woke from my daze briefly. 'When did you know it was you?' I asked Adam.

'I knew right from the start…almost.' He gave a careless shrug, but his gaze was probing. 'It was right there in my second envelope—the one we got straight after the murder.'

Marcus gave the pair of us a disdainful look. 'I don't know…' he said, in a slightly petulant tone. 'I think this young lady might have had a slight advantage over us when it came to solving the case.'

I knew he was thinking about the larder incident, and just letting my consciousness touch the edge of that memory was enough to make me tremble deep down in my core.

But Marcus was wrong. In the situation I found myself in now, I had no kind of advantage. No kind of advantage at all.

I slipped away while the others were still debriefing themselves, using the excuse that I had to go and pack up the clothes that were no longer needed.

Izzi had been generous enough to offer the clothes she'd bought to their owners, and most of the guests had elected to keep their outfits. I collected the evening wear that wasn't in use and made sure it was hung up or packed properly for their journey home. Once that was done I still had the 'spares' to deal with. The extra clothes would return with me to Coreen's Closet, where they'd go back on the rails.

I was hanging up the wonderful red velvet dress when I heard a soft knock at my bedroom door.

People in love are supposed to thrill at the thought of their sweethearts, aren't they? So why did the adrenaline surge that hit me incite the fight-or-flight reflex? I looked across to the window. Unless I wanted to shimmy down a two-hundred-year-old drainpipe I only had one choice.

Rather than shouting an invitation to come in, I walked across the room and opened the door a crack, keeping most of myself behind its pro-tective bulk. My eyes widened. It wasn't Adam standing there, but Nicholas.

'Can I come in?' he asked, looking very serious indeed.

I stepped back, way back, and opened the door wide. He walked through and, after a second of hesitation, closed it behind him.

'Is something wrong?' I asked.

Nicholas stopped looking grim and his face broke into possibly the most beautiful smile I'd ever seen on a man. The sort of smile that undoubtedly turned the knees of countless society darlings to custard. All the more devastating because it was one hundred percent genuine. My knees, however, remained decidedly un-custard-like.

'I wanted to thank you,' he said, and when he spotted my raised eyebrows added, 'for all you've done this weekend.'

I frowned. 'I didn't do much, and besides Izzi's paying me. It's work, really.'

'No, not just that,' he said earnestly. 'For being so great to Izzi.' He paused and glanced towards the closed door, and lowered his voice. 'I know she gives the impression she's indestructible...'

One side of my mouth lifted. It was obvious,

despite her loopiness, that he clearly loved his sister.

'Izzi has a lot of "friends"—I think *parasites* might be a more appropriate word—who hang around for what they can get out of her.' He looked down at his shoes. 'I'm ashamed to say that when I first met you I thought you were one of those people who'd take advantage of my sister's gregariousness and generosity. I was wrong.'

Now it was my turn to look at my shoes. I *had* been guilty of that, or at least it had been that way in the beginning. I looked up again, to find him regarding me carefully.

'You proved me wrong, went the extra mile.'

I'm not usually in the habit of stopping someone layering on the compliments, but this girl he was talking about? I'm ashamed to say she was nothing like me. I shook my head. I was the girl who thought of herself first and others second.

'No,' I mumbled. 'I don't think you understand.'

Nicholas was smiling again now. 'I think I understand well enough.'

I turned back to the bed, where I'd flung the red dress, and picked it up. It was something to do to hide the heat creeping up my cheeks.

'That's a beautiful dress,' he said.

'Yes.'

I fetched a garment bag and began putting it inside.

'Perhaps you'd consider wearing it out one evening...if you'd like to have dinner with me, that is?'

I literally had no words. Nicholas Chatterton-Jones was asking me out? Really?

'Why me?' I blurted out. 'I've seen the world you live in, the people you mix with. I wouldn't fit in.'

He considered that for a moment. 'I know...but perhaps that's the key. I always seem to go for the same type of girl...'

Didn't I know it? I listed it out for him. 'Beautiful, rich, thin—'

'You're beautiful,' he said plainly.

Before, I would have lapped that comment up, demanded more, but I took his compliment with the same simplicity it had been given. 'Thank you.'

He walked over to the bed, so we were standing either side of it. 'You shouldn't put yourself down.'

I laughed out loud as I walked over to the hanging rail and deposited the red dress in its protective cover there. He really didn't know me at all, did he?

'Oh, I don't think you have to worry about that!' I said, still giggling as I walked back to the bed. 'But if it makes you feel any better I will add one more thing to the list. One thing I'm definitely not.'

He pressed his lips together in an amused grin and raised an eyebrow.

'Duck-faced,' I said, and then wondered if I'd taken things too far again.

Nicholas chewed this over. 'You know,' he said finally, a look of surprise lifting his features, 'I hadn't realised it, but I think you're right!'

We both laughed then. He really was even more good-looking when he laughed. What a pity that his cheeks were missing a pair of roguish dimples, that his eyes weren't chestnut brown, and that the sparkle that should've been there in them just wasn't.

'I've decided everything on that list is decidedly dull, anyway,' he added. 'I've certainly seen the attraction of a woman who has a little *more* to her.'

If he was talking pounds and inches he'd better duck, because a right hook was coming his way.

Thankfully, he saved himself with his next words. 'A woman with pizzazz and sparkle.'

Ah, despite the show of loyalty to his sister he was still talking about the minx, and she certainly had all of that. Problem was…I wasn't sure that girl existed in her pure, undiluted state any more. She seemed to have been watered down with some truly awful qualities—like compassion and bravery and honesty. Really, what was I going to do with her?

'So how about it?' Right now Nicholas looked the least stuffy and laced-up I'd ever seen him. He nodded towards the clothing rail. 'You, me, the red dress and a table for two next Saturday?'

There was an awkward silence, and he must have read the confusion on my face—I'm really going to have to do something about that—because he gave a resigned smile.

'I'm too late, aren't I?'

I bit my lip and picked up the next item of clothing, but I didn't say anything. I wasn't quite ready to face what I felt for Adam yet, let alone admit it to anyone else. It didn't matter, however. I think my traitorous face had said it for me. Nicholas cocked his head, the way an old-fashioned gent would have done when he doffed his hat to a lady, and then retraced his steps to the door.

'Ring me if you ever change your mind...'

I just smiled weakly at him, clutching what I now realised was Adam's dinner jacket to my chest. He gave me one last smile and closed the door, leaving me marvelling that, despite the horrendous timing, my minx-like attempt at *less* was the *more* Nicholas Chatterton-Jones wanted.

Pity the minx had left the building.

You know that elephant that everyone always says is standing in the middle of the room? Well, it hitched a ride home with us on Sunday evening. Adam was all calmness and civility on the outside, but his dimples had ironed out and his driving was even more atrocious than usual. I didn't say anything. Because of the elephant, of course.

He stopped at Coreen's Closet and helped me unload everything into the back room, then he drove me to my flat and helped me carry my suitcase up the stairs to my front door.

As he was leaving he said, 'I'm going to Malaysia on Thursday, to do the finishing touches on the hotel project.'

I blinked and smiled. 'How long will you be away?'

'Two weeks.'

I nodded. Not because I was agreeing to anything but because I needed to do something. 'How nice,' I added, after I'd bobbed my head far too many times to look sane.

Nellie must have decided to stay in the car, because he gave me a long, searching look and then said, 'Come with me.'

'What happened to no pressure? To giving me time to think?' I snapped.

The sparkle in his eyes was dim now. He looked tired. 'Maybe some time alone together is just what we both need?'

It all seemed so reasonable. So reasonable, in fact, that it made my skin itch. I gripped the edge of the door. 'That's not quite right, though, is it? You don't need any more time to figure it out.'

He was silent for a few seconds, and then he

confirmed all my worst fears. 'I want you in my future, Coreen.'

A future. Long, endless days stretching into the greyness ahead of us. An infinity in which we would grow old, tire of each other. I didn't ever want to get tired of Adam, and while we'd been friends I never had.

I arranged my features into a neutral, serene expression. 'I'll always be in your future, Adam. No matter what happens between us.'

His jaw jutted forward just a millimetre and he licked his lips. I knew he could read the words 'brush-off' in my tone and body language. I was counting on it, in fact. I didn't want to spell it out in words.

The horrible thing was, I knew he would take it slowly if I asked him to. He would put my wishes—my needs—above his own. Unfortunately, I was scared, and it turned out I just wasn't that big a person.

'What are you saying?' he asked slowly. 'Are you trying to tell me you don't see anything changing between us?'

I threw my hands in the air. 'Yesterday we were just good friends. Now everything's been turned on its head. I don't want to be rushed. I have to be free to make my own decisions.'

'What you mean is that you have to be in control.'

'No! That's not true.'

'Yes, it is.' He stepped forward into the flat and I spun around and marched into the living room ahead of him. If we were going to have a good old ding-dong we might as well do it in private. My downstairs neighbour thought I was strange enough as it was.

Adam followed me. 'Yes, control. That's why you make all those poor saps who follow you around dance on their hind legs. As long as you're in control, you're safe. But love isn't like that, Coreen. Love means giving a piece of yourself away, trusting someone else with it.'

I folded my arms across my chest and hugged my elbows. 'You're talking about love, but I think you're forgetting I haven't worked out how I feel about you yet.'

'Haven't you?'

So we were back to this game, were we? We both knew how we felt about each other, and we both knew that we knew…It wasn't just tiring any more. It was dangerous.

I had already worked out that Adam wasn't above playing dirty, and now he blew my carefully constructed denial to smithereens. He was suddenly across the room, his arms around me, his mouth only a whisper away from mine.

'Tell me to stop if you don't want this,' he said softly.

I closed my eyes, trying to think of the words to do just that, but anything as simple as *no* or *stop* had exited my vocabulary by the back door, and the only things left were unintelligible sounds and lengthy explanations I sadly didn't have time for.

I didn't do anything as his lips began to move on mine. Okay, well maybe I did *something*. But how is a girl supposed to stop herself from wrapping her arms around a man when he's kissing her like that? I'd defy any one of you to do better. I had to kiss him back. To do otherwise would have been rude. Maybe I took it too far by running my tongue along the edge of his lip, but I've always had a problem with that.

The problem with a kiss like that one was that I

wasn't stage-managing it. Usually I set the pace. I controlled how much and how hot. I played the part of vintage minx to the max, in other words. But with Adam I wasn't playing anything. I didn't even have my usual costume of red heels and even redder lips. Adam wasn't kissing the minx; he was kissing *me*. I felt the shockwaves right down in my soul. They lapped at the shore of my identity, eroding it, rearranging it, as the surf does the pebbles. And I could sense a tidal wave on the horizon—one that would overwhelm and devastate.

I untangled myself and stumbled back. Adam reached out a hand to steady me, but he didn't override my decision to stop. Neither of us said anything, but as the seconds dragged on his expression grew both softer and darker. I was transparent again, I could tell.

'You can trust me,' he said quietly, emphatically.

Oh, I knew I could trust Adam. Adam was practically manufactured from the stuff. Despite the fact I'd been dazzled by a sexier, more dangerous side to him in the last few days, I knew that if you sliced him open, like sugary seaside rock, he would say 'loyal and true' right to the core. It was *me* I couldn't trust.

'I know what you're thinking,' he said. 'What you're afraid of. But love isn't total surrender. It isn't one person sacrificing themselves totally for another.' He glanced at the black-and-white picture of my mum on the mantelpiece. '*Real* love isn't like that. It's a two-way street.'

I looked at the photo of Mum. She'd been about twenty when it had been taken and she looked so jaunty and happy, strolling down the road with her cute little mini-dress and her big sunglasses pushed up on her head. Before she'd met my dad. Before he'd sucked the life out of her. I'd bet she thought love was a safe pastime too.

When I turned my attention back to Adam I had a shock. He looked so like the boy who'd used to promise me he'd always look out for me with that grim sense of earnestness that only youth can provide. My lips trembled and my insides churned. I wanted so much to believe him, but there were things he hadn't thought of…

When you gave that little piece of yourself to someone else for safekeeping, how did you know when to stop? How did you know if you'd given too much of yourself away? Once it was gone, there was no getting it back. And I knew just how destructive that kind of imbalance in a relationship could be. Had seen it first-hand.

I took a step back—mentally, at least—and let out a dry laugh, causing Adam to frown.

This was me we were talking about, wasn't it? The girl who manipulated people, situations, just about anything, to get what she wanted. The girl who knew everything about taking and nothing about giving. I was just Scrooge in a circle skirt and eyeliner. Surely if anyone was safe from my mother's fate it was me?

But that left me with another problem.

I walked over to my retro, cherry-red fake leather sofa and sat down with a bump. 'Why on earth do you want me, anyway, Adam?' I kicked off my shoes and dug my toes into the shaggy rug. 'I play games, I'm demanding and selfish…' For the first time that evening I looked him straight in the eye. 'The truth is, I don't know if I'm even capable of the kind of love you're talking about.'

He came and sat beside me, took my hands in his and made me look at him. 'It's the girl who disguises herself in the vintage clothes who does all of those things. The girl who practises her walk. The girl who is never seen without her trademark crimson...' He dragged the pad of his thumb across my bare lips. 'But I'm not in love with that girl. You don't *need* to be that girl with me.'

A tear slid down my face. And then another, and another. He really meant it. He loved me that much, and I didn't deserve it. A space inside myself that I hadn't even realised was achingly empty started to fill up. And with the fullness came more tears.

I don't know how long I cried, but Adam just held me, whispered soft words into my ear: he believed in me, he knew what I was capable of, and it was much more than I gave myself credit for. Eventually, worn out, I hiccupped to a halt. Still Adam didn't move. I was so exhausted I started to drift in and out of a leaden sleep. I was only vaguely aware of him moving away and fetching the duvet from my bed, of him draping it over me and kissing me tenderly on the head. I fumbled for his hand and found his trouser leg instead.

I didn't care; I held on with all the strength I had left.

'Don't go,' I mumbled. 'Stay. I need you.'

There. The first time I'd ever said those words to another human being. I'd never admitted to needing anyone before. Ever. Not even my mother. Especially not my mother.

Adam didn't hesitate. He just squidged down next to me on the sofa, pulled a corner of the duvet over himself and wrapped me up inside him. I wanted to touch as much of him as possible, to imprint his warmth on as much of my surface area as I could, and as sleep began to fog my mind once again I reached for his fingers and tangled mine with his.

And then I drifted off to sleep. Holding Adam's hand.

Warmth. Touch. Those were the first blissful sensations I was aware of early the following morning. Adam's fingers still loosely entwined in mine. His breath, warm and even, at the back of my neck as he lay spooned behind me. I tightened my fingers round his, lifted both our hands towards my face and softly kissed his knuckle.

He must have stayed awake long after I'd suc-
cumbed to dreams, because he was sleeping
heavily now and I slid out of his hold fairly easily.
There was a slight snuffle and a twitch as I stood
up, but I tucked the duvet back around his neck
and he drifted off again.

I didn't leave the room straight away, but stayed
there, watching him. Why that prickling at the
top of my nose was back, I wasn't sure. Maybe
it had something to do with the fact that I felt as
if I wanted to empty myself of everything I was,
everything I ever would be, and pour it into him.
The urge was so strong it was a physical sensation, welling up inside me, threatening to burst
through the very pores of my skin.

I'd been wrong about not being able to love
Adam the way he wanted me to. As I stood,
unable to tear my eyes from him in the lemony
dawn light, I knew I was my mother's daughter.

Just before I tiptoed out of the living room, feeling raw and vulnerable, I grabbed Mum's photo
off the mantelpiece and hugged it to my chest.
I took it with me and laid it on my bed before
heading for the bathroom. After all that luxury
I was desperate for the comfort of my own sur-

roundings, my own temperamental shower that I knew just how to get the best out of, my haphazard and kitsch decorating style, with scarves over lampshades and classic movie posters on the wall.

When I came out of the shower, wrapped in a fluffy red towel, I paused and picked up the photo I'd left on the bed. The image of my mother, smiling and carefree, blurred. I hadn't known her like that. Of course I'd seen her smile and heard her laugh, but I'd been too young to remember much of the time my parents had been together. After my dad had left, even if her face had been making all the right adjustments to portray happiness, it hadn't rung true. There had always been that moment when she finished laughing, a pause when the sadness would seep back in, a moment when she returned to her default state.

I wish you were here, Mum. I wish you could tell me what to do.

But she wasn't here. And the desire to have her with me was just yet another fantasy. While she'd been alive she'd only been half present in my life, both physically and emotionally. I kissed the tip of my finger and pressed it onto her smile.

I love you, Mum, but I can't be like you. Sorry.

I placed the frame on my bedside table and got dressed, choosing my favourite black pencil skirt and a hot-pink wing-collared blouse, finished off with raspberry suede heels with roses on the toes. I twisted my hair into a French pleat, but left my blunt fringe loose, so it hung above my eyebrows like a curtain. The jet-black liner went on with little flicks of my wrists to create wings, and with each sweep of rich and luxurious lipstick across my lips I felt my power returning.

When I'd finished I walked into the hall to check my reflection in the full-length mirror. I looked like me again. But not the frivolous, carefree version of myself I had expected to see. The glimmer of fun in this Coreen's eyes had hardened into iron.

I picked up my patent black handbag and took one last look around the living room before I left. It was far too early to open up the shop, but I needed a walk, some time to clear my head. Adam was still unconscious, but this time as I looked at him the welling sensation didn't return.

I blew the sleeping Adam a kiss, ending with a little finger wave, and then walked out of the room and left my flat, my shiny black handbag swinging from my finger in synchronisation with my hips.

I turned the sign on the door of Coreen's Closet to 'Closed' and sighed. I was very tempted to rest my head against the cool glass and let it soothe my aching brow, but Alice was watching me. She'd been watching me all day.

She was standing behind the counter, checking the till. I turned back to face her and gave her a wide Crimson Minx smile.

'Out with it,' was all she said.

I rolled my eyes.

Despite the swirling pregnancy hormones, my business partner was still able to pin me down with a look. 'I mean it. How did the weekend go?'

I blinked innocently. 'I've already told you all about it.'

Alice made a dismissive noise. 'You told me about the *fashion*. Now I want you to tell me about the *weekend*.'

'Oh,' I said airily as I walked jauntily back to the cash desk. 'Nicholas Chatterton-Jones only asked me to dinner, that's all.'

Instead of squealing and dancing round the shop with me, Alice folded her arms. 'And…?'

I shrugged. 'And I'm thinking about it.'

'Now I know there really is something wrong.'

I sagged against the counter, resting my well-padded behind on its edge, and blew out a long breath. It made me look like a horse, but I was past caring. Alice started packing things into her handbag, but I knew appearances were deceptive. She wasn't going anywhere until I spilled my guts. Sometimes my willowy red-headed business partner was decidedly unbendable.

I crossed my ankles and fixed my gaze on a sequinned silver jacket that Gladys, our one-eyed shop dummy, was wearing. 'I think I might be in love.'

'With Nicholas?'

I didn't answer. Couldn't.

How could I make my feelings concrete with words when I knew I was about to behave despicably? Alice waited in silence, and I was just on the verge of screaming when someone gave the locked shop door a hefty shove.

Adam.

He was peering over the top of the 'Closed'

sign, the afternoon sun tinting the tips of his messy-but-sexy hair gold. I held my breath to stop myself from running over to the door, yanking it open, flinging my arms around him and burying my fingers in that shaggy mop. I didn't. My butt was frozen to the counter and I let Alice waddle over to the door and unlock it instead. She had steel in her eyes when she turned back. Steel and knowledge.

Oh, heck. I was rumbled.

'Well, I'm off, then,' she said breezily, grabbing her bag and swinging it over her shoulder. She kissed Adam on the cheek as he entered the shop, and then waddled out of the door, pausing briefly to turn back, smile meaningfully at me and let me have her parting shot.

'Be good.'

I smiled weakly back, not promising anything, because I knew I wasn't about to be anything but very, very bad.

CHAPTER ELEVEN

Cry Me A River

Coreen's Confessions
No more confessions. There's nothing left to tell—except for how the story ends…

ALICE disappeared, and the compact and cluttered shop floor of Coreen's Closet fell silent. I didn't know what to say to him. However, Adam proved just how much he could say without pesky things like words getting in his way. The twinkle in his eyes—my twinkle—blazed out at me. Pretty soon it spread to the corners of his eyes, causing them to crease, and then it worked its way down to engulf his mouth. I was tempted to dive into that smile and lose myself in it.

'Hi,' he said, his voice low and warm. I reminded myself this was a Monday afternoon. I had no business thinking about Sunday mornings.

'Hi,' I said back.

We looked across the shop at each other.

'Do you want to grab something to eat?' he asked.

I sucked a mouthful of air in and held it in my lungs. 'Maybe later.' I glanced back at the open door to the office. 'I've got some things I need to catch up on. After the weekend...'

It made me feel worse that he believed me.

'Hold that thought!' he said, his smile widening further. Then he walked over to me, dropped one sweet, intoxicating kiss on my lips and strolled out of the door.

After locking the door behind him, I went immediately to the washroom and reapplied my lipstick, and then I decided I ought to find *something* to do.

I found a couple of boxes to unload and reload, rooted around in my desk drawer for a lost stapler, and then rearranged my costume jewellery in its wood and glass display case. I was just about to turn my attention to the hatpin display when the door rattled. I didn't have to look round to know who it was, and I didn't need to ask what it was in the carrier bag he was holding—

I could smell the delicious waft as soon as he entered the shop.

He plopped the bag down on the counter and headed straight through to the back office, flung his keys down on the desk and fetched the pink picnic hamper. I coughed before he unbuckled it, and he looked up.

'Fish and chips?' I asked, wrinkling my nose slightly.

The smile dropped from Adam's face. 'You don't want fish and chips?'

I shook my head and clasped my hands low behind my back. 'Actually, I have a hankering for Thai.'

He looked at the tightly wrapped paper bundles in the carrier bag. 'But it's hot, and I asked for onion vinegar especially for you.' He started to unwrap the paper and a delicious acidic waft hit the back of my nose. Saliva pooled underneath my tongue.

I gave him my big-eyed 'little girl' look. 'I really fancy Thai,' I said, the lie sliding effortlessly through my evenly spaced teeth.

'You're sure about this?' Adam gave the hot

bundle of fish and chips a longing look. I nodded and blew him a kiss.

There was no eager yip, as one of my 'puppies' might have given, but he sighed and rubbed his hand over his face. I knew he was going to do it for me—not because I'd pushed him into a corner, but because his innate sense of chivalry had kicked in. 'Okay, Thai it is.' He shrugged. 'At least it's only a few doors down.'

I bit my lip.

On purpose.

'What?' he said, his voice heavy.

'I don't like that restaurant any more.' I lowered my head a little and looked at him through my lashes. 'I like the Blue Dragon.'

'But that's the other end of town!'

I did my coquettish little one-shouldered shrug. 'You did say you'd get it for me...'

He gave me a long, hard stare, and then he picked up the hamper and disappeared into the back office again. While he was gone, I pinched a couple of chips from one of the parcels, stuffed them into my mouth and then quickly rearranged the packet so it looked as if none were missing.

My, those chips were good. Heavenly, in fact. I closed my eyes and licked the salt off my lips.

I had to swallow quickly when I heard Adam returning, minus hamper but in possession of his car keys. Something inside me sank. This was what I'd wanted, but a part of me hadn't wanted it to be this easy, hadn't wanted Adam to be predictable like all the others.

I was leaning against the cash desk, arms bracing me, and he peeled one of my hands off the shiny surface, turned its palm upwards. 'I don't play games and you know that,' he said as he dropped the keys into my waiting palm. 'If you want curry from the Blue Dragon, you're going to have to get it yourself.'

My skin began to prickle. Damn it. I liked this new Adam with the menacing edge to his voice too much.

Okay, he might not have been as predictable as I'd both feared and hoped he would be, but that didn't mean I was going to let him outmanoeuvre me. I pushed the keys against his chest and let go. He caught them on a reflex.

'I'm not driving that hulking machine of yours

'round these narrow streets,' I said, glaring at him and stood up. 'Fine. I'll get my dinner myself.'

'Fine,' he said, glaring back at me.

I didn't really want to, but what choice did I have? I picked up my purse and stalked out of the shop and up the road to the Spice Heaven. Ten minutes later I was back, with a curry I didn't really want.

Adam had moved into the back room, but his chivalry thing had decreed he wait for me. A parcel of fish and chips was waiting unopened on his lap. As soon as he saw me he dived in. I set to work opening my plastic tubs and dishing rice and curry onto a pink plate.

Adam wasn't 'twinkling' so much now. He stared at his fish and chips in silence. It didn't look appetising. But then cold fish and chips never do.

I ate a bit of my food, and then resorted to pushing it around my plate and taking the odd nibble when I felt Adam's eyes on me—which was more often than not, unfortunately. Coconut milk and onion vinegar definitely did not make a good taste combination. This was no comfortable silence we were enjoying. I knew he was thinking hard, trying to work out what his next move would be.

'I'm off in three days,' he said as he bit into a chip, grimaced and dropped it back into the open parcel on his lap. 'You sure you won't change your mind and come with me? I think you'd really enjoy it.'

This was not just an invitation. I could tell by the wariness in his eyes that it was a test. I dabbed at the corner of my mouth with a pink paper napkin and shook my head. I needed Adam to go away on his own. This whole thing was going to be so much harder to accomplish if he didn't.

He put his parcel down, stood up and walked across to where I was perched on the edge of my desk.

'Please don't, Coreen.'

I pretended not to understand. 'I don't *do* humidity,' I said blithely, and attempted a cheeky smile. It wasn't a good attempt. It stayed in place, but it felt as if it was only hanging there by a thread.

Adam took the plate out of my hands and put it on the desk behind me. 'I told you that you don't need to be this way with me. You don't need to be *that girl* with me.'

And there, in a nutshell, was the problem. Because I really did need to be that girl with Adam. It was the only way I could keep myself intact. So if he didn't want me this way then maybe he shouldn't have me at all. I raised my chin a notch.

'It's who I am, Adam. If anyone knows what I'm like, you do.'

Liar. Coward. Those two words rang in my ears as I watched him digest what I had just said.

A siren sounded somewhere on my desk. My phone. My current ring tone was the song *'The Girl Can't Help It'* from the Jayne Mansfield movie of the same name, police siren and all. I never missed my phone ringing any more, but it drove other people nuts.

I retrieved it, grateful for an excuse not to look Adam the eye for a few seconds, but when I saw who it was calling I sent him straight to voicemail. Adam stared at me.

'That was Nicholas,' I said lightly, keeping a close watch on his reaction. 'He's not such an idiot after all, it seems. The plan worked. He wants me to go to dinner with him on Saturday evening.'

Reaction-wise, I got more than I bargained for. I don't think sound escaped Adam's lips, but he looked as if he were snarling. 'Coreen…'

I slid my phone closed and smiled brightly at him. 'Even Nicholas came to heel in the end. Just goes to show that no man is completely untrainable.'

Except Adam.

'Stop it, Coreen.'

I don't think my expression held quite the right level of innocence and guilelessness that I'd aimed for. Probably because everything inside me seemed four times heavier than normal. Even my face felt heavy. 'What do you mean?'

He turned his head. Too disgusted to look at me, I guessed. I pretty much felt the same way.

'I know what you are doing.'

And I knew that he knew. But I couldn't stop. It was the only way to save both of us from a lifetime of heartache.

I didn't say anything. I'd planned to tell him I was going to accept Nicholas's offer of dinner, but it turned out even I wasn't despicable enough to do that. It's nice to have a least one redeeming feature: Coreen Fraser, not *quite* pond scum.

There was no point in lying any further, anyway. Adam knew Nicholas was just a diversion. He stood up, towering above me as I rested against the desk, only inches between us. Close enough to reach out and touch if I was stupid enough. Weak enough.

Soft fingers curled around my chin and pushed it upwards until I had no choice but to look at him. That's when the tears started to fall, running down my cheeks and trailing down my neck, each one following the track of its predecessor. Adam's expression softened. It was as if something in his eyes had opened and I could see deep down inside him, see all the treasure I'd been half-blind to all these years. Strength. Courage. Loyalty. All the qualities I lacked.

I knew my feelings for him were written clearly over my face, because I saw a spark of hope in his eyes. I couldn't let it live. I tensed my jaw and the last pair of tears fell. With every ounce of my strength I arranged my features into blankness. I wound up my shutters, pushed him away without even moving. Without even breathing.

He saw it too. And I wished he hadn't opened those windows to let me see inside, because now I saw it all turn to ash. I saw the desolation, the rage, the pain. I knew I was breaking both his heart and mine.

He stepped back, shell shocked, and I realised that up until that moment he'd never considered that there would be anything but a Happy Ever After for us, even if I had to be dragged into it kicking and screaming. That light, that welcoming light, the one that had always been there for me in his eyes, sputtered and disappeared.

Something really had been murdered this weekend. And I was the one who'd killed it.

I realised that holding all the power, having that ultimate control I had always craved, tasted nowhere near as sweet as I'd imagined it would. In fact it made me sick to my stomach.

Now Adam's shutters came down too. He picked up his car keys, clenched them into his fist, and gave me one last rigid look. I knew those windows would never open again. Not for me, anyway. The thought of them doing so for another girl one day almost drew a cry from my lips, but I held it back, finally getting a handle on the 'controlling my face' thing.

Adam turned and walked away. Out of the shop and out of my life. I realised that somewhere in the back of my head I'd foolishly thought he'd eventually forgive me for this one day. After all, I was only being *me*. Vintage Coreen. He'd always forgiven me before. But as I ran to the doorway that led to the shop floor and hung on to the frame I saw him stride away down the road and realised he never would. I'd taken it too far.

I stood there motionless, hardly breathing, my fingernails folded into my palms. It would have been a good time for the violins to play, to swell around me in melody sweet and sad and sharp enough to make hearts bleed, but I made yet another discovery: there was nothing romantic about moments like this.

Nothing romantic at all.

A limousine arrived to pick me up at seven on Saturday evening. It took me over the river, wove skilfully through the London traffic and deposited me at an exclusive little restaurant in the

West End. I was fussed over and shown to a table, where Nicholas was waiting for me.

He rose as I approached and kissed my hand. From anyone other than Nicholas I would have thought it was too smooth to be true, but he really was like that all charm and effortless manners.

'You look stunning,' he said as he pulled my chair out for me.

'Thank you.'

I did look good. I hadn't worn the red dress, though. I'd chosen an Audrey Hepburn-esque little black dress and put my hair up. Nicholas liked the pared-down minx, after all, and it didn't go to give a man the impression he had even the tiniest bit of control over what a girl did. The lipstick was crimson, of course, but I'd faltered when it had come to the shoes.

I'd looked at the array of different styles and shades of red in the bottom of my wardrobe, had tried loads on, but discarded them all. I'd ended up nipping over to the shop and borrowing the black suede evening shoes with the bow on the front. But I was so used to wearing nothing but red on my feet that every time I looked down I had the feeling that something was wrong. They pinched my little toes as well, but what the heck?

As you can tell, I reverted to the original plan after Adam left.

Okay, *straight* after Adam left I stumbled home, ate two pints of Devilish Diva chocolate ice cream, watched three black-and-white movies back-to-back and then sobbed into my pillow until morning. But that had been five whole days ago now, and despite the fact I had repeated the process on the two following nights I had forced myself to get up and move on. Hence the plan.

It had been a good plan, after all.

Adam had been right—I was ready for something more serious than puppy-training. I was ready for a serious relationship. With someone like Nicholas. Someone who thought *that girl* was funny and sparkly and full of pizzazz. Someone who couldn't see through the dizzying parade of polka dots, who couldn't make them transparent with just one look.

Only…

As we ate the exquisite food and chatted in the candlelight I kept looking at my Perfect Man and noticing lots of silly little things.

The fan of creases at the side of his eyes, for one. They didn't appear often enough, and when they did they didn't make me feel like melted marshmallow inside. The eyes were all wrong, of course. Too clear. Too blue. No cheeky little glimmers inside that dragged the corners of my mouth up, whether I liked it or not. And I just kept wanting to lean across the table and unto his top button, or muss his hair up a little. Sometimes perfection can be a little too uniform.

I sighed. I was being picky, wasn't I?

Deep down, I knew why. Deep down, I tried to tell myself all about it. But somewhere nearer the surface I squished it down again—a kind of mental sticking of the fingers in one's ears and singing 'la-la-la', I suppose.

Nicholas topped my glass up with fizz that was a hundred times better than the stuff I usually got at the corner shop.

'Coreen?'

'Mm-hm?'

'Is everything okay?'

I flashed him my Marilyn smile. 'Absolutely wonderful.'

He glanced over his left shoulder. 'You seem to

be fascinated by something behind me. Is there something wrong with the restaurant? And you keep sighing.'

'No.' I shook my head emphatically. 'The restaurant is lovely. I wasn't looking at anything in particular…' Not in these elegant surroundings, anyway. But I was hardly going to own up to the mental slide show that had been distracting me.

Adam's grin as he stole yet another sweet and sour pork ball.

His face close to mine as he adjusted a pair of hideous tortoiseshell glasses.

The look in his eyes as I sang my mum's favourite song.

I put those thoughts away and shuffled through the images of the previous weekend, trying to find a nice one of Nicholas—like the time when he'd congratulated me on geeing everybody up, or when he'd asked me to dance—but they were all fuzzy and out of focus.

I let out a breath, long and slow. Nicholas's eyebrows dipped at the edges. Maybe he'd been taking lessons from Robert. He looked down at his architecturally beautiful dessert and then up at me again.

'I'm still too late, aren't I?'

I tried to deny it, but the words wouldn't come. Dissolved by the fizzing bubbles of the vintage champagne, no doubt. Nicholas, gentleman that he was, said nothing further. He was charming and interesting as we finished our meal, attentive and amusing during coffee and on the limo ride home. The kiss he pressed on my cheek as we parted was decidedly platonic.

I stood with my key in the lock and watched the limo pull away into the starlit summer night. Not once did I sigh. I felt like Cinderella in reverse. I'd gone to the ball only to wind up with the pumpkin. No, that wasn't fair to Nicholas. He was everything I'd imagined him to be.

It was just that he wasn't *my* pumpkin, and no amount of wishing would make it otherwise.

I held up fine until I got into the flat and ran to the kitchen, but as I opened the freezer and reached for yet another tub of Devilish Diva I paused and my fingers numbed on its frosty surface. Seemed I was going to bypass the ice cream stage and fall headlong into the sobbing stage. Gluey tears, a waterfall at the back of my nose and some rather unattractive snorting noises to follow.

I pulled the ice cream tub out of the freezer, clutched it to my chest, and then closed the freezer door, turned around and slid down it until I was sitting on the kitchen floor.

Why did it still hurt? Why did it hurt *more*? I hadn't made the fatal mistake of following him. I was doing the right thing, wasn't I?

Suddenly I got really angry. I dropped the ice cream and stumbled to my feet with all the grace of a new-born giraffe, kicking off the uncomfortable black heels as I did so, and ran into the living room to stare at the picture of my mother, back in its proper place on the mantelpiece.

'It's all your fault!' I screamed. '*You* did this to me. This is *your* legacy and I don't want it! I don't want it!' I picked up the frame and hurled it across the room. It hit the fake zebra skin rug and shattered. I made a horrible gurgling noise down in my throat—it could have been the word *no*, trapped by the raw swelling there—and then ran over to the frame. Shards of glass lay on the floor, but the wood was still intact. I smiled. And then I cried. And then I cried harder.

Carefully, I bent down to pick it up and shook the loose glass onto the floor. Then I held it in both hands, my knuckles paling, and stared down at her. Although the laughing face never changed, her expression seemed to sober. I searched her eyes out and locked on to them. Laughing eyes, I reminded myself. Happy eyes. I didn't want to see anything else.

But even that didn't work. Clouds passed over the eyes too. It was as if she was looking back at me, trying to send me a message.

Don't be a fool like I was. Don't make the same mistakes I did.

'I'm trying not to,' I whispered, my voice thin and high. 'But it's not working. I just feel… I feel…' I closed my eyes and wept silent tears. There was no point in denying it to myself any longer. No point in trying to wedge my blinkers back on my stubborn head.

I was in love with Adam and I always would be.

But it wasn't in my genes to balance. Two-way street? Hah! Anyone who knew me understood that I hogged the road and behaved as if I had my own personal police escort when I drove. And it would be no different in love. As whole-hearted as I'd been at bending the world to my will and making it serve me, I'd show the same total commitment to loving Adam.

I knew I could give to him and never stop giving. Never stop until I was a grey shadow of myself, just as my mother had been. And then I wouldn't be the woman Adam had fallen in love with any more. That's when the rot would set in.

Oh, he'd stay at first. I didn't doubt that. Adam didn't disappoint, after all. But we'd stagnate, grow to hate each other, and he deserved so much more. So much more than a woman who would always be waiting for the moment when she found the note on the mantelpiece, when she found a dent in the pillow but the bed cold and empty…

If there was one person I couldn't be Left Behind by, it was Adam. So maybe it was better that I'd taken fate into my own hands and *chosen* the moment we'd part, rather than having it thrust upon me years from now, when I'd been lulled into a false sense of security.

I risked a look at Mum. She was smiling again, eyes laughing. Had I imagined the rest?

Couldn't you have found a nice man? I whispered mentally. *A good man who wouldn't have abandoned you and sucked you dry? A man with a safe pair of hands to hold your heart? Then you might still be here. I might have had you long enough to—*

A safe pair of hands.

Oh.

I wasn't sure whether I was frowning or smiling, and a nerve in my cheek worked overtime as it tried to decide which one.

I was *just* like my mother, but it had taken me up until now to understand all that that meant. All that it *could* mean.

Perhaps my red suede ballet pumps hadn't been the way to go. I know the boat driver had recommended sensible footwear, but for me this *was* sensible footwear. I'd heard Langwaki was a tourist hotspot, so I'd expected it to be quite cosmopolitan, but I hadn't realised just how many islands there were in the archipelago. While some had bustling resorts, the island I was speeding through a turquoise sea towards was apparently home to only one hotel.

My hair, however, had lived up to expectations, so I wasn't totally wrong-footed.

I soon forgot all about the frizz, though, because the scenery was stunning—full of mountainous islands covered so completely in rainforest that only a sliver of pale yellow at the water's edge broke up their unrelenting green caps. I turned to look out of the other side of the boat, not wanting to miss a thing, and realised we must be nearing our destination. Rather than skimming past the closest island we were heading straight for it. As we rounded a jutting headland the resort came into view. I think I may have stopped breathing.

This was no ordinary hotel. It wasn't the rough, wooden, tree-hugging backpackers' base I'd imagined either. No, this…this was more like an exotic fairytale.

As far as I could see along the shore were wooden chalets on stilts, their legs in the water, some of them more than one storey, all with pointed red-tiled roofs. From the midst of the cluster of waterborne buildings a walkway jutted out towards us, with a larger structure on the end. The boat docked beside some steps that led up to what I now realised was a reception area, and the other passengers began to disembark.

I let them flow around me.

This was obviously a luxurious and well-established resort. Was I really in the right place? I checked the name with the boat driver and he nodded emphatically. I had no choice but to ascend the stairs and carry on my journey.

I arrived in the reception area and headed straight for the wide, glossy, dark wood reception desk. A young woman in a smart collarless red jacket smiled at me. I cleared my throat.

'I'm looking for Adam Conrad? He builds—'

'Ah, yes. Mr Conrad. I will arrange for someone to take you to him.'

She clapped her hands twice and a lad in the same uniform appeared from nowhere and motioned for me to follow him. I trailed along behind him, listening to his commentary in accented English on the hotel, its history, the fauna and flora of the island, and how excited everyone was about the new eco-friendly treehouse development on the resort. I just nodded vacantly as I followed him through a maze of walkways that linked the chalets and then finally led onto dry land, over the top of a silky white beach and on into the jungle into a section of the resort that wasn't yet open to visitors.

After a few minutes we stopped at a plank bridge strung over a small ravine, which led to yet another stilted wooden chalet on the other side. But where the other chalets had been a traditional Malaysian design, this had a flowing, organic shape. Modern, yet beautiful.

My guide pointed across the bridge and nodded, then scampered away back towards the ocean.

I inhaled, then gently planted my ballet pumps on the bridge. It didn't lurch or swing and I picked up speed. The canopy of leaves high over my head let in pale golden light. I knew the jungle was probably the same here all year round, but to me everything looked fresh and recently sprouted, ready to bud.

As I reached the chalet I saw it was merely another mini-reception area. From this point the bridges and walkways headed off into the trees in different directions. There was no polite young lady in red behind the desk this time, but a foreman in dirty work clothes.

'I'm looking for Adam Conrad,' I said.

He nodded, then pointed to the walkway on the far right.

'Thank you.' I began to walk again, and this time the planks took me upwards into the trees until I reached a platform that circled one of the larger trunks. Two further walkways sprouted from this platform. Which way now?

I looked back at the man in the hut and he made giant arm gestures, pointing me right yet again. I kept my eyes on my feet as I climbed higher, but after a handful of steps I stopped and let out a loud gasp.

The ground had dropped away beneath me. Down below I could see a stream, rushing over the rocky hillside towards the beach. There was even a small waterfall, framed with ferns. I shook my head slowly in amazement, but when I looked up even that stopped. In front of me was the most amazing thing I'd ever seen. A whole village of treehouses, dotted here and there in the jungle, some big, some small, all of them similar pleasing organic shapes, and all connected by a lattice of rope bridges, platforms and walkways. The design was asymmetrical, yet oddly harmonious.

Every pod-like chalet was set a short distance

from the main walkway and could be reached by flowing wooden steps. Some had only short flights. Some curled round the trees like spiral staircases.

I spun around on my heels, taking it all in, letting the circular motion create a breeze where there was none, ruffling through my simple fifties sundress and cooling my skin.

I could hear voices, but I wasn't sure where they were coming from. One of the treehouses close by, I thought. I set off, keeping my ears trained on the sound. Listening for Sunday morning.

I stopped when the voices were directly above me, in one of the treehouses that could be reached by a spiral staircase. A man appeared at the top of the steps and I waited until he was halfway down before I approached him.

'Hi,' I said, and he almost jumped three feet in the air. I suppose he wasn't used to seeing frizzy-haired women in white sundresses wandering round the jungle. 'I'm looking for Adam Conrad.' He replied in broken English and pointed up the winding staircase. I smiled my thanks and climbed up.

The main room of the treehouse was stunning.

Even though this part of the resort was still officially under construction, it was obviously very close to completion, because it was fully furnished and decorated. In the centre of the room was a large bed, covered in crisp white linen, surrounded by a dark-stained wood and cane frame. The walls were also white, and though such a stark colour scheme should have looked bare, the golden-green light from the jungle outside spilled in through a large opening at the far end, making the room seemed fresh and clean and inviting.

My ballet pumps made hardly any noise as I crossed into the centre of the room, looking all around.

'Adam?' I only whispered his name, overcome by a sudden attack of nerves. I had no idea how he'd react to my arrival on his territory. If I'd been him I wouldn't have wanted anything to do with me.

For a moment all I could hear was the fluttering of the sheer white curtains that half covered an open space on the far side of the room, but then I heard a creaking noise outside, and as I looked more closely I realised there was a balcony built onto the edge of the room, joining it with the jungle outside, making it seem as if one flowed into the other.

And then I saw him. Adam. Standing by a wooden railing, gazing out into the unending foliage. I walked up to the threshold until I was half in, half-out of the room, my suede-clad feet silent on the polished wooden floor. But as I stepped out onto the balcony I let my foot slap down, announcing my presence.

Adam spun round and his mouth dropped open.

I'd thought I couldn't ruffle Adam's feathers, thought I'd lost the knack, but I'd never seen him so off-balance. It went deeper than momentary surprise, however. His face seemed different. The lines were etched in harder and there were smudges of darkness under his eyes.

My nose stung furiously. *I'd* done this to him.

I'd thought I understood how much I'd hurt him, but until this moment I hadn't. I really hadn't.

'Hi,' I said, and my heart clog-danced against my ribs.

I couldn't hold his gaze. Stupidly, I'd thought I might see a flicker of the old warmth there, but there was nothing. I'd never realised brown could look so cold and uninviting. I couldn't keep my greedy eyes off him for long, though. As much as it hurt, I had to let them feast on him. It felt as if I hadn't seen him in months. In years. But I suppose that fitted. I'd spent a whole lifetime *not seeing* Adam Conrad. How stupid and cowardly and selfish I'd been.

'What are you doing here?' he said quietly, not moving—as if doing so would cause me to vanish in a puff of smoke.

I took a step forward. 'I missed my best friend.'

He closed his eyes and then slowly opened the lids, his body sagging slightly. 'I'm not sure you and I can ever be friends again,' he replied carefully.

I was being stupid, edging my way up to what I wanted to say to him, and my first clumsy attempts had made it sound as if this was all about what *I* wanted, what *I* needed. It's just that I was terrified. Terrified I really had taken things too far this time—beyond the point of no return—and that I'd destroyed the one thing I treasured most in the process. I didn't deserve his forgiveness, but I had to try.

'I know,' I said in a quiet voice. 'But while

you've been away I've had time to think. Really think.'

Adam gave me a look that said he wasn't sure 'thinking' would solve my problems. A swift kick in the pants, maybe…

I moved closer, until I was almost at the balcony railing with him, but the sentence I'd planned fluttered away as I took in the view.

Because of the steep hillside we seemed to be floating in the air. Before us was the jungle—tall trees, waxy-leaved plants, the odd bright spot of colour—and beyond that, just visible through the dense vegetation, the white gold of a beach, topped by a shimmering sea.

'I think this is the most beautiful place I've ever seen,' I whispered.

Adam turned away from me again and placed his hands on the railings. 'I said you'd like it.' His voice was flat and expressionless, but at least he was talking to me. He talked towards the jungle, keeping his gaze straight ahead. 'What do you want from me?'

I swallowed. This was it. All the games, all the side-stepping and self-protection had to end now. Telling the old Adam I cared for him would have been hard, but confessing it to the new Adam…it was nigh on impossible. This Adam was far more dangerous—and not just because I'd opened my eyes to the attraction that had been so very obvious to almost every other woman he met.

This Adam had the power to crush me, to turn me into that pining, hopeless woman I'd never wanted to be. Where old Adam would have grudgingly forgiven me eventually, this man I loved probably wouldn't. Probably *shouldn't*. But he had my heart anyway, and I knew that if I was ever going to have the slightest chance of repairing things with him I needed to offer it to him as a sacrifice. If he plunged a knife in it, so be it. I was helpless to do otherwise.

I matched his position at the railing, staring out over the lush greenery as I collected myself, but after a few heartbeats I turned to face him and waited until he looked round. He didn't turn fully, just glanced warily over his hunched shoulders and stiff arms.

'I'm sorry,' I said, and darn it if I didn't start to cry again. What was wrong with me these days? I took a moment to hold the flat of my finger under my eyelashes, mopping up the moisture, and to still my trembling mouth. When I pulled my fingers away they were moist and grey. 'I really am sorry…for all the things I said, all the things I did. All the things I *tried* to do…'

I inhaled, collecting my courage together.

'But I also came to tell you that you are wrong.'

I saw a flash of surprise in Adam's eyes, swiftly replaced by anger. Surely that had to be better than nothing, than the deadness I'd put there? I carried on, feeling braver. 'Love *isn't* a two-way street. Love *isn't* about balance.'

He stood up and opened his mouth to contradict me, but the words died on his lips as I reached out and curved my palm around the side of his face, as I smiled into his eyes. He froze beneath my touch, and I knew I might be making the biggest fool of myself ever, but I couldn't stop now. There were things that needed to be said.

'Love *does* mean total surrender, because…'

I let my fingers brush across his cheek, his jaw, the contact thrilling me, connecting me to him. A pulse of electricity travelled all the way up my arm and detonated somewhere in my chest.

My voice was watery when I spoke again. 'Because there is no balance in the way I feel about you, Adam Conrad. No balance at all. And it scares me…' my voice wobbled and croaked '…so much.'

Still no thaw. Still no swirl of caramel in those hard eyes. I felt my stomach sink to the jungle floor, way below us.

'The way I feel about you… It's all that I am. It's *everything*. I finally realised what my mother's true legacy was, why I'm proud to be like her.'

He held my gaze, gave me a moment to gather my next words.

'Just like her, I have the capacity to give my heart fully and completely. Without reservation.' My face crumpled slightly. 'She didn't choose well, though. But I have. I've found a very safe pair of hands for my heart.'

In one swift movement Adam pushed himself up from leaning on the railing and pulled me into his arms. We stood forehead to forehead, chest to chest, our hearts thudding against each other.

'I love you, Adam. More than life itself.'

I kissed him—slowly, softly, sweetly—on the lips, for the first time with the full knowledge of how I felt and what that meant. No more hiding, no more running. He didn't respond at first, and I wondered if, despite his feelings for me, he might never be able to trust me with his heart in return. I really didn't deserve it, after all.

And then I pulled back and waited, my hand still curved around his cheek. It seemed as if my heart had closed its eyes and counted to a hundred before he reacted, before I saw any change at all in his features.

His eyes melted and his hand closed over mine. He peeled my fingers from his face. He turned my palm over and graced it with the softest kiss. He opened his mouth, but I pressed a finger to his lips.

'I haven't finished yet,' I said.

Adam smiled behind my finger, his eyes on fire, and his lips squashed into strange shapes as he tried to talk. 'I love it when you get all bossy with me.'

I ironed out my answering grin and became serious again. 'I'm giving everything to you because I know you will give the woman you love all of yourself in return.' I placed my hand on his chest and stared at my fingers there. 'This good heart is strong and loyal and faithful, and I wondered if, one day, you might trust me enough to make it…' I risked a look up at him and said with a trembling voice, 'Mine?'

Adam gave me a look so intense I thought the soles of my shoes would melt. Then he cupped his hand behind my head and kissed me until it spun.

'Always yours,' he said softly, his smile swinging back into place. 'Always was, always will be.'

That was all I needed to know. I grinned back.

His gaze roved over me, drinking me in. 'I see *that girl* hasn't completely disappeared.'

I shook my head. 'You wouldn't have it any other way. Life would be very boring if she wasn't around to keep you on your toes.'

He let out a gruff laugh. 'I see we're going to have to work on that one.'

He didn't say any more, just stared at me, and I stared back at him. There was a whole conversation going on between our eyes, but I had no idea what language it was in. I didn't much care, because while my mind didn't understand the words, my heart had caught his meaning and was nodding in agreement.

Adam brushed his thumb across my bottom lip. My eyelids fluttered shut and I let out a sigh.

'I see the red lipstick is here to stay,' he said.

I tipped my head back and parted my lips further, ignoring his comments and replying with an invitation of my own. When he didn't respond I cranked one eyelid open slightly.

'Yep. It's staying,' I said, a smile warming my lips. And then I closed my lids again. 'But you have my full permission to kiss it off any time you like.'

He chuckled. But, Adam being Adam, didn't disappoint.

* * * * *

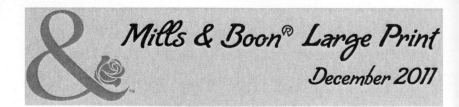
Mills & Boon® Large Print
December 2011

BRIDE FOR REAL
Lynne Graham

FROM DIRT TO DIAMONDS
Julia James

THE THORN IN HIS SIDE
Kim Lawrence

FIANCÉE FOR ONE NIGHT
Trish Morey

AUSTRALIA'S MAVERICK MILLIONAIRE
Margaret Way

RESCUED BY THE BROODING TYCOON
Lucy Gordon

SWEPT OFF HER STILETTOS
Fiona Harper

MR RIGHT THERE ALL ALONG
Jackie Braun

1111 Rom LP

Mills & Boon® Large Print
January 2012

THE KANELLIS SCANDAL
Michelle Reid

MONARCH OF THE SANDS
Sharon Kendrick

ONE NIGHT IN THE ORIENT
Robyn Donald

HIS POOR LITTLE RICH GIRL
Melanie Milburne

FROM DAREDEVIL TO DEVOTED DADDY
Barbara McMahon

LITTLE COWGIRL NEEDS A MUM
Patricia Thayer

TO WED A RANCHER
Myrna Mackenzie

THE SECRET PRINCESS
Jessica Hart

Mills & Boon® Online

Discover more romance at
www.millsandboon.co.uk

- 🌹 **FREE** online reads
- 🌹 **Books** up to one month before shops
- 🌹 **Browse our books** before you buy

...and much more!

For exclusive competitions and instant updates:

 Like us on **facebook.com/romancehq**

 Follow us on **twitter.com/millsandboonuk**

 Join us on **community.millsandboon.co.uk**

Visit us Online | Sign up for our FREE eNewsletter at **www.millsandboon.co.uk**